The
Princess
and the
Pauper

Look out for:

The Virginity Club

Coming Soon!

The Princess and the Pauper

Kate Brian

SIMON &
SCHUSTER
LONDON

First published in Great Britain in 2004 by
Simon & Schuster UK Ltd.
A Viacom Company
Africa House, 64–78 Kingsway, London WC2B 6AH

Originally published in 2003 by Simon & Schuster Books for
Young Readers, an imprint of Simon & Schuster Children's
Division, New York.

 Produced by 17th Street Productions,
an Alloy company
151 West 26th Street, New York, NY 10001

A CIP catalogue record for this book is available from
the British Library

ISBN 0689860714

1 3 5 7 9 10 8 6 4 2

Printed by Cox & Wyman Ltd, Reading, Berkshire

Prologue

Night skies in L.A. seem to stretch out for ever, sending their warmth out to the entire world, rolling above the ocean and reaching the countries on the opposite shore. I imagined the air I was breathing right then drifting into Vineland, a country I knew so much about but had never seen.

I could barely believe I was really standing here on this balcony, looking up at the familiar night sky – the *only* familiar thing around me.

My jeans were gone (with a floor-length black silk dress in their place), my hair was dyed (from ferret brown to shades of glossy gold), and my black plastic watch had been replaced by strands of glittering rubies. I could just imagine my mom's reaction if she saw them. 'My God, Julia. Look at you,' she'd say. 'One of those bracelets is worth more than I make in five years.'

Of course, I wasn't Julia that day – I was someone else.

And it wasn't even about the dress, the hair, or the bracelet.

I glanced quickly at Markus Ingvaldsson, son of Vineland's minister of cultural affairs. He stood next to me on the balcony and looked out towards the Pacific. His hair was messy from the wind and flopped in his face, and the arms of his tuxedo were a tiny bit too short. I looked down at his hands, beautiful hands with long, slim fingers. On his middle finger he wore the signet ring that had been handed down through the generations. *Handed down through the generations.*

The closest I'd ever come to owning something with that much history was when I'd bought a pair of used Roller Blades at a garage sale.

Markus caught my gaze and started to smile, revealing the adorable small dimple on his left cheek.

That was it – I was turning to mush inside all over again. And it was all wrong. Foreign dignitaries' sons were supposed to be stuffy and boring and pretentious. They weren't supposed to have strong arms, and they weren't supposed to have dimples! Because . . . well, because . . .

Because I wasn't supposed to fall for anyone.

According to Mom, not to mention *YM* and all the shows on the WB, falling for a guy is exactly what sixteen-year-old girls *are* supposed to do. But when you're trying to maintain your grade point average while figuring out a way to make sure you and your mother don't get evicted, you don't really have a lot of extra time to spend stressing about the new hottie who works at the Circle K. So I had reached my age, sixteen, without ever having had a boyfriend, a serious crush, or even a guy to go to the movies with. And that was just how I'd wanted it.

How I *still* wanted it . . . right?

Markus's smile widened, the dimple got deeper, and I

blinked, then took a step back from him and returned my gaze to the view over the balcony.

I could see the lights of the Palisades and almost make out the dark waves of the Pacific Ocean. I'd waded out in that ocean many times. I'd jogged along the bike path that ran along the beach. I'd lain in the sand and tried to get an even tan, never quite getting it right.

Inside the French doors that led to the ballroom, people were dancing in Armani tuxedos and rich jewel-toned silk gowns to music played by a string quartet. The air smelled like a mix of fresh flowers and expensive perfume. Everyone was perfectly relaxed, perfectly calm. Everyone except for me. How could I be calm? I was in big trouble.

Just a little while ago Markus and I had waltzed together inside that room. The other dancers had cleared the floor to watch us, admiring the graceful way we moved together. And even that was a lie. In my regular life I wasn't graceful at all. I was always running into lockers, tripping over kerbs, and spilling coffee down the front of my shirts. But not tonight.

Suddenly I shivered, even though the breeze against my face was warm and soft.

'Are you cold?' Markus asked, moving closer to me.

'No,' I said, in a voice I'd practised in front of my mirror, my cat staring at me in confusion as I struggled to get the slight tinge of an accent just right. 'I'm fine.'

Markus stepped closer anyway and laid his hand over mine where it rested on the railing. His hand felt huge. I could barely breathe – I felt like fifty genetically altered butterflies were flying around inside my stomach.

Don't mess this up, I told myself, fighting to stay in control and get my heart rate back down. 'It's – it's beautiful out here,' I managed to choke out, my voice shaking slightly.

'Yes,' Markus agreed. 'It is.'

And then I did it, the stupidest thing I'd ever done in my life: I looked into his eyes.

I knew it was a cliché, I knew it with every fibre of my being, but Markus's deep blue eyes were more amazing than the sky, the Pacific Ocean, and every other beautiful thing and person I'd seen tonight all rolled up into one.

My knees *actually felt weak.*

Markus met my gaze and smiled again, then reached his hand up to touch the side of my face. 'And you,' he said softly. 'You're pretty beautiful yourself.'

Okay. I was going to vomit on him and pass out. But then, that probably wouldn't have been too princessy of me.

Of course, princesses probably aren't supposed to blush, either. Unfortunately, I had a feeling that at that moment there wasn't an inch of my skin from my scalp down to my toes that wasn't bright red. Was this night the best night of my life or the worst?

'Markus— ' I started to say, then stopped myself.

'Hmm?'

'Nothing.' I bit my lip.

'Do you want to go back in?'

'No,' I blurted. *Oh God.* I'd said that way too quickly. Was it okay for a princess to sound so over-eager?

'Let's just stay out here for a couple more minutes,' I added in what I hoped was a more casual tone.

He moved his hand across my face and brushed a few loose strands of hair behind my ear. I gripped the railing tighter.

'Are you sure you're okay?' he asked. Then his mouth straightened into a line and his brow furrowed. 'I know what this is about,' he said, sounding more serious than he had all night.

My breath caught. 'You – you do?' I squeaked.

He nodded. 'It's because I was talking to that other woman earlier, isn't it?'

I stared at him, wide-eyed, torn between a blast of relief that he was still clueless and total confusion about what he was talking about. What woman?

'I assure you, Fröken Vandelkoff means nothing to me,' Markus continued.

Fröken who? I gave a slight nod, trying to look as solemn about the whole thing as he did.

And then it was back – Markus's perfect, crooked grin. 'Besides, she's what, sixty-five? And also, I think she might be a distant cousin.'

I couldn't help it – I started to giggle. I didn't care if princesses giggled or not; there was no way to stop.

Markus laughed, too, and then before I knew it, his arms were around me and he was pulling me towards him.

'You're so . . . different tonight,' he told me, his mouth so close I could feel his breath on my face.

'Mmm,' I agreed, not trusting myself to say anything more. 'This whole night has been completely unreal,' I murmured into his chest.

'And is that so bad?' Markus asked gently.

Before I could answer, he leaned down and kissed me. The kind of kiss that ends all kisses. The kind in the movies. (The good movies, not the cheesy ones with Freddie Prinz, Jr.) The kind of kiss that makes you forget about strange hair and old shoes and eviction notices and everything else that doesn't mean anything.

Finally the kiss ended, and we stood staring at each other.

Oh, Markus, I thought. *If you only knew who I was or what I've done to you, you would never kiss me again.*

Chapter 1

From: princessgirl@vineland.org
To: rockmyworld@aol.com

So it's all set! I am coming to America in just one week! How great is that? I'll finally get to meet you and hear you play in person. I'm so excited, I almost can't believe it! :-)

Love,
C.

From: rockmyworld@aol.com
To: princessgirl@vineland.org

c —

girl — i so wish you would tell me your real name . . . my band is reel excited about the festivel . . . its' definitely going to rawk . . . and it's so cool too meet a girl from another country!!! so does this mean your parents agreed to let you come to the concert???

later babe!
ribbit

Ribbit

Don't you worry. My friend Ingrid is going to America with me and she is very smart and she will find a way to get us there. So just count on us showing up! Can't wait to–

The door swung open, and I looked up quickly from my laptop. *Ugh*. One of the main problems princesses have (besides tiara hair, which is worse than pillow hair, believe me) is queens. That is, mothers. Mine stood in the doorway, looking very tired in a lavender satin gown.

I don't mean a gown like a ball gown. Princesses and queens don't wear those except for, well, balls, or ceremonies, or really important dinners. I mean gown as in nightgown. Yes, that's right. Royal people wear nightgowns and pyjamas just like regular people. And sometimes we wake up in the morning with drool crusted around our mouths (of course, we have servants who make sure we never go out in public like that).

My mother stood in the doorway. Her face was free of drool, but she had big dark circles under her eyes. For the past few months she'd been nursing my grandmother, who had diabetes and was apparently really sick. Lately my mother was exhausted pretty much all the time.

'What are you doing?' she asked, leaning against the door frame.

'Nothing.' I minimised the e-mail window on my

8

screen, then shut the laptop and put it down on my mahogany night table.

My mother frowned, then came in and sat down on my bed. California, my cat, meowed angrily and leapt onto the floor. California was a Persian and hideously spoiled. Like me, he had the best grooming a country of two million people could offer. Unlike me, he actually enjoyed it.

'Your father has been delayed. As you know, he was supposed to return home from England tonight.' My mother sighed, patted her ash blonde bob, and looked around the room like she didn't know what else to say.

'Delayed, wow,' I said, rolling my eyes. 'How totally shocking.'

There was an awkward pause.

'Well, if you're bored, we could send someone out to Video International,' she finally said. 'I don't know if I could stay awake for a whole movie. But maybe if we got something short . . .'

It used to be that when my father was away, my mother and I would spend the night hanging out together. We'd get the cook to make us chocolate milk shakes and we'd watch American TV shows on the satellite dish or get one of the staff to rent us an American film. We only did this when my father was out of town. He thought American movies 'taught bad values'. I thought America looked fabulous – it was obviously so different than Vineland, full of models and astronauts and gangsters and people trying to kidnap the president. A few months ago my mother and I would have been all set up in front of the projection screen, watching one of those movies together. But not any more.

'Whatever. I don't feel like a movie,' I said. 'I was going to go to bed early anyway.' I faked a yawn.

'All right, dear. Whatever you say.' She couldn't hide the relief in her eyes, and I felt a small, familiar twinge inside.

It seemed like every day my mother and I grew farther apart. She'd been busy taking care of her mother, and I'd been busy writing e-mails. And feeling sorry for myself, which my mother completely did *not* understand. She'd married my father when she was my age, sixteen, and missed out on having any of the exciting adventures teenagers are supposed to have. But she didn't seem to mind. She thought the occasional Josh Hartnett movie should be enough excitement for any princess, and whenever I complained about being bored with my life, it was like she took it personally.

So after a while I started keeping my thoughts a secret. My thoughts . . . *and* my relationship with Ribbit.

It was actually kind of cool – I was just like Buffy back when she had to hide her whole secret slayer life and the Angel thing from her mom (only I wasn't killing demons or anything).

My mother cleared her throat. 'Carina, your father really would have loved to be here with us tonight. I hope you know that.'

'Yeah. Just like he would have loved to have been here for pretty much my entire life.'

'Carina, it wasn't his fault. There was a storm coming in England, and it was unsafe for the jet to take off. He's staying at the queen's tonight, and he's been asked to attend the queen's jubilee, so he won't be back until tomorrow night.'

'I wanted to go to the queen's jubilee! Skull Boiler is playing there!'

'Is that the one with the devil-worshipping lead singer?'

'Mother,' I said, rolling my eyes. 'Please. *Everyone* has pentagram tattoos these days. You're being ridiculous.' A few months earlier my friend Ingrid had smuggled me some goth CDs in classical music cases. They were so intense I couldn't believe it. Imagine the freedom to be so loud and dark and say whatever you wanted.

The Goth Princess of Vineland. I liked the way that sounded.

I picked my biology textbook up off the floor and flipped through the pages, pretending to read something about the make-up of a cell while my mother stared off into the distance. I hoped she would go away soon so I could get back to my e-mail.

But for once, she wasn't in a hurry to leave.

'So, the Ingvaldssons are going to be at that embassy ball they'll be holding in the States while you're there,' she said. She tried to force a smile. It looked totally fake. 'Markus will be there.'

Unbelievable. I was going all the way to America and I still couldn't get away from Markus.

My parents and Markus's parents were good friends. Markus's father was the count of Vasta and minister of something-or-other in our government. And Markus and I had played together when we were, like, four. He'd really liked the wooden blocks, while I was more partial to the glitter glue.

Markus wasn't a bad guy or anything, but our parents had been trying to throw us together for years. Markus was exactly the kind of guy every mother wishes for for her daughter. He was respectful and well mannered and always laughed appreciatively whenever anyone made a bad joke. He was the kind of guy middle-aged women always describe as 'a real catch'.

In other words, he was completely and totally boring.

Especially when you compared him to Ribbit – Ribbit was so exciting and sexy and *real*. He sang songs with loud meaningful lyrics. And didn't worry so much about following the *rules* all the time.

'I don't want to talk to Markus,' I said.

'Dear, he just wants to get to know you better.'

I hated it when my mother called me 'dear'. It just reminded me all over again how straight she was, how straight and stuffy my whole *life* was. I shook my head and started chewing on my nails.

'Please stop biting your nails,' my mother said. 'It's an unbecoming habit.'

That was another thing. I was so sick of always having to be 'becoming'. I wanted to wear ripped jeans with safety pins in them. I wanted to snort when I laughed. I wanted to slouch.

I stopped chewing. 'I want to meet *new* people when I'm in the United States. There will be plenty of time to get together with Markus after I get back from L.A.,' I said. I felt so cool, calling it L.A. instead of Los Angeles, just like they did on TV. I tried to keep my voice level. If my mother knew how much I was looking forward to this trip, she'd get suspicious and make me stay home. She never wanted me to have any fun.

'Dear, are you sure you're ready to do this goodwill tour on your own? Maybe I should go with you after all.' She reached out and tried to stroke my hair, but I ducked out of the way.

If Mother came, there was no way I'd ever be able to bend the rules and meet Ribbit.

'I'll be fine,' I said quickly. 'And you can't leave Grandmamma when she's so sick. Don't worry, Mother. You know I always do exactly what I'm supposed to do.' *Even when what I'm supposed to do is incredibly boring,* I added silently. 'Besides' – I rolled my eyes – 'Killjoy will be around.'

'Carina, don't be cruel. Fröken Killroy has served the royal family with great dedication for many, many years. She cares deeply for you.'

Fröken Killroy was the palace 'handler'. She was just like a prison guard, but she got to wear better clothes. I had a lot of nightmares about her, where I was a parrot in a cage and she shoved food pellets through the wire. One time I got to bite her finger.

'Mother, you know Ingrid and I will be with our delegation at all times. I don't know why Fröken Killroy even needs to be there.'

My mother sighed. 'Dear, Los Angeles is a big, frightening city.'

'Frightening?' I snorted. 'Frightening how?'

'Well . . .' She thought a minute, and California stared at her, like he was waiting for tales of ferocious dogs dropping out of the palm trees. 'I hear there are gangs in Los Angeles that make signs with their hands' – my mother folded two fingers down and waved her hand around to demonstrate – 'and I also hear that the cars go too fast and that there are crazy Roller Bladers on the beach. And I know all that smog is terribly unhealthy. Take shallow breaths.'

'That all sounds fabulous,' I blurted. My mother's eyes widened, and I wished I'd kept my mouth shut.

'You're only sixteen, dear. Try not to grow up all at once.'

'I just feel . . .' I trailed off.

'Feel what?' she prodded, her voice softening.

I sighed. 'Never mind. Whatever. Just forget it.' California crawled onto my lap and I threw him off the bed. He sent me a killer glare from the floor. I glanced up and my mother was giving me the same look.

'Carina, I don't know what's happened to you lately. I really don't.' My mother sighed, too, and stood up. 'You haven't even asked about your grandmother.'

'I was just about to,' I said quickly. The truth was, I had barely seen my grandmother these past few months, and I hadn't visited her yet in the hospital. There had just been too much on my mind. 'How is she?' I asked.

'Not very well, I'm afraid. She could use a visit from you.'

'I'll see her as soon as I get back from my American tour,' I promised.

She raised her eyebrows. 'Keep that promise. And not just because it's your duty as princess to set an example of proper behaviour. Someday you'll be in her place, and you'll want your grandchildren to visit you, too.' With that she left the room.

I narrowed my eyes at the door. Lately pretty much all of my conversations with my mother left me feeling the same way – incredibly annoyed but at the same time a tiny bit guilty. Did she *always* have to remind me of my duties as a princess? Did everything have to come back to that?

I fell back on the bed, reached over to the windowsill, and found my Walkman. I put the headphones on and clicked a button, and Ribbit's voice filled my ears.

> *Girl, you're the only one who understands*
> *I like peeling Elmer's glue off my hands*
> *You girl are so hot*
> *When I touch you I need an oven mitt*
> *I need to drink a quart of your spit*
> *You're as sizzling as the sun without an umbrella*
> *I'm the pizza crust*
> *You're the mozzarella . . .*

I smiled in spite of myself. Okay, so maybe the spit part was gross, but so what? He was an artist; artists were supposed to be more passionate than other people. And in only a matter of days, everything I'd hoped for would come true. Freedom and sand and surf and palm trees and Toadmuffin. I knew I wouldn't be able to sleep if I thought too much about it, and in 1764 a law had been passed in Vineland that banned princesses from getting less than eight hours of sleep a night. Okay, not really, but Killjoy always clucked her tongue when I dozed off during my lessons, and if my father saw me looking tired, he'd yell at me about my eating habits and protein and callisthenics. Callisthenics? Who even *said* that?

I took off the headphones and pressed the silver button next to my bed, which was connected to a buzzer in the servants' quarters. A few seconds later my maid, Asha, appeared at my door.

'Princess,' she said.

'Asha, I'm going to need my white silk pyjamas from my wardrobe. And tell the kitchen to send up a mug of hot chocolate.'

'Yes, Your Highness.' She handed me my pyjamas and trotted down the hall towards the kitchen.

'And tell him to use a combination of dark *and* milk chocolate,' I called after her. 'It's too bitter otherwise.'

I got into my pyjamas, and then I changed my mind about the hot chocolate, so I hung my Princess Sleeping sign outside the door. Ingrid had given it to me as a joke, but it came in awfully handy sometimes.

As soon as I turned out the lights, my cell phone rang. I groped around in the dark until I found it.

'Hello?'

'Carina.'

'Who is this?' I joked.

'It's Ingrid. Your best friend.'

'Hmmm, doesn't ring a bell.'

'I'm the one whose bad attitude is covered up by her insincere respect for all authority. You know, the only person who provides light and joy in your otherwise cold, sad existence.'

'Ah, yes. I know you. So what's up?'

'Well, for one thing, right now I am cowering in the dark just beyond the back wall of your property. I looked over the wall a few minutes ago, and the guards are sneaking cigarettes somewhere. The coast is clear.'

'Ingrid, it's late,' I said. I wanted to lie in bed and think about Ribbit.

'Ingrid, it's late,' Ingrid said, in a perfect imitation of me. She groaned. 'When did you turn a hundred and five, Carina? Get out here.'

I started to respond, but then I realised she'd already hung up. I went to the window, opened it, climbed through, and manoeuvred my way down the trellis. It was covered with a kind of wisteria that bloomed, strangely, in the month of September rather than in the early spring. Every now and again my toes would catch one of the lavender blooms and tear it loose from the vine. By the time I hit the ground, there was a little carpet of them nestling on the soft green grass.

I crept barefoot across the palace grounds towards the great stone wall, careful to look for signs of the guards. Once, the year before, they had caught me sneaking out and had taken me back to the house to be confronted by my parents. My father had been home that night – big shock – and had just enough time to tell my mother she needed to control her daughter before a helicopter landed on the back lawn and flew him off to France. I had been grounded for two weeks, which was bad enough, but had also been denied e-mail, which was a torture not even the old kings of savage countries could have dreamed up.

When I reached the back wall, I moved the branches of a bush aside and found a toehold in the granite wall. I reached up and found some fingerholds, too, guiding myself over and dropping down on the other side.

The moon was full overhead, and a breeze that smelled of lavender blew across my face. Ingrid, who liked lavender cologne, was lurking nearby. Ingrid was pretty, in her own way. She had short blonde hair and very wide eyes and full lips. But she was really skinny, and she had big clumsy feet. Her mother was that way, too, and her grandmother. And how can you fight a bloodline? Believe me, I had tried.

Ingrid wasn't royalty, but her family and mine went way back, friends since the eighteenth century. Like me, Ingrid was an only child. Like me, she thought her parents were kind of lame. Like me, she was sick of her boring, over-protected life. Like me, she thought Markus was duller than biology. We had a lot in common.

'Ingrid!' I called in the darkness.

I felt a pair of hands cover my eyes. 'Guess who?' Ingrid whispered in my ear.

'Beats me.'

Ingrid's hands fell away from my face and she started walking ahead of me into the forest, motioning for me to follow her.

I liked walking around barefoot at night. It made me feel free. The moon was full and bright overhead, and our feet barely made a sound as we brushed through ferns and banks of silky grass. We were headed to a little clearing in the woods that had two flat rocks right next to each other. We called the place the Sanctuary, and that was where we went when we snuck out in the middle of the night – which, these days at least, was something we did pretty often. Out there it was possible to believe we could get up and walk back to normal houses in normal parts of Vineland, where a girl didn't have to know how to hold a fork, or curtsy, or move with grace, or go on hospital tours. (Don't get me wrong – it's not like I don't feel sorry for sick people. But I hate the smell of hospitals, and the flashbulbs going off in my face, and nurses coming up to shake my hand. And I hate having to read incredibly boring books to patients who always seem to be coughing on me.)

We reached the rocks and sat down. Ingrid was wearing a cream-coloured tunic shirt and raw silk trousers that I'd never seen before. Unlike me, Ingrid loved all those dainty haute couture clothes I had to wear. 'That's the thing about you, Carina,' she always said. 'You don't appreciate all the perks of royalty. I should have been a princess instead of you.' She didn't mean it in a harsh way. She was just being honest.

Ingrid pulled a pack of imported Silk Cut cigarettes out of her trouser pocket and lit one with a gold Zippo. She took a long drag, and the light from the end gave her face an eerie glow. She handed the cigarette to me. I inhaled and immediately began to cough. And cough. And cough.

I knew the benefits of cigarette smoking – rebellion against authority, making your parents angry, and masking the odour of the rose-scented cologne a princess is supposed to wear. The problem was, I hated smoking. But I found that kind of embarrassing, so I did it anyway.

Ingrid clapped me on the back. 'You all right?'

'Ahhh.'

She took the cigarette back. 'Oh, I forgot how *delicate* princesses are,' she said, laughing. 'So.' She paused to take another long drag. 'Did you hear from that Toad guy yet?'

'His name's Ribbit,' I said. 'And his band is called Toadmuffin. Toad*muffin.*'

'Yeah, right,' said Ingrid. 'I looked at their web site. "The Circus Will Weep When I Kill All the Clowns." Brilliant, really.'

'That doesn't mean kill for real, you know,' I said. 'It means metaphorically. Like "My Girl Is a Rainbow Wearing Tight Shirts".'

'Ooh, metaphorically,' Ingrid said, laughing. 'I see.'

'Ribbit and I were e-mailing each other earlier tonight,' I said.

'No way!' said Ingrid. Even though Ingrid could be a little bit mean at times, she sounded genuinely happy, which I thought was really sweet. She thought I could do much better than Markus.

She took one more puff on her cigarette, ground it out on the edge of the rock, and threw it on the ground. 'So what did he say?'

'Oh, you know, just that he was excited to meet me and all that.'

'Did you tell him who you are yet?'

'Sure, Ingrid. "Look for me, princess of Vineland. The

20

girl who makes Rapunzel look free." No, of course I didn't! He still thinks I'm a normal girl, and that's what I'm going to be when I meet him.'

'Suuure. A normal girl . . . pulling up in a chauffeured Mercedes-Benz, accompanied by a scary-looking old woman who will make sure you two stand three feet apart at all times.'

'It's not going to be like that. I'm going to find a way to get rid of Killjoy – and the chauffeur, too. And you're going to help me.'

'I don't know,' Ingrid said. 'I'm still in trouble for that rope ladder and fake passport I gave you for Christmas. Somehow your parents took it the wrong way.'

I laughed. 'Come on, Ingrid,' I said in my best whiny voice. 'If anyone can figure out how to help me get away from Killjoy, it's you. It'll be like that movie *Escape from Alcatraz*. I rented it one time with my mother. All these prisoners escaped from jail by making their own raft and sailing away. It's a true story.'

'Your point?'

'Escape is possible.'

'Well, if Killjoy had been the prison warden, those three guys would be sitting in cells right now. *And* they would know how to curtsy. '

'Ingrid, I'm serious.'

'All right, all right. I'll think of something. It's worth it just to get you away from Markus the Boring.'

'His family is going to be at the embassy ball in L.A.,' I said.

'Oh yeah?'

'Hopefully I won't get stuck talking to him all night like I did last time.'

'Seriously. He's so dull he makes me want to vomit.' Ingrid rolled her eyes. 'So, what's the first thing you're going to say when you finally meet Ribbit face-to-face?'

'I'm going to say, "Hi, I'm the girl you've been e-mailing."'

'What name are you going to use?'

'I don't know. I'll make one up.' I had got Ribbit's e-mail address through our head of cybersecurity. I hadn't exactly bribed him, but I had made some calls and ensured that his daughter was admitted to the most exclusive girls' school in all of Vineland. There are times when being a princess has its benefits.

The breeze was cool against our skin. The stars overhead shone bright. Ingrid and I squinted up at them. I wanted one of the stars to suck me out of my kingdom and then set me down again in L.A.

'It's going to be so incredible,' I whispered. 'Palm trees, sand in our toes, iced tea that tastes like raspberries, surfers, movie stars, dancing all night. Supposedly there's some beach where everyone walks around completely naked.'

'Naked?' Ingrid said nervously, sounding totally un-Ingrid. 'Maybe I'll get Killjoy to dig me a big hole and I'll bury myself with just my neck sticking out. I'll pick up guys that way. Then I'll dig myself out after they've already fallen in love with me.'

'Look, the point is, L.A. is completely unlike anyplace we've ever been before, and I don't want to waste it at a bunch of boring receptions, eating salmon croquettes and listening to someone blab on and on about what an honour it is to stand next to me. You have to help me, Ingrid. We need to come up with a serious plan.'

'I'm thinking, I'm thinking.'

I looked up at the stars again as Ingrid lit another cigarette. 'Seven days from tonight and we'll be there,' I said. 'In seven days we'll be in an entirely different world. In beautiful, glamorous L.A. . . .'

Chapter 2

. . . In beautiful, glamorous L.A. it was seven o'clock in the morning and I, Julia Johnson, woke up to the sound of dripping water. It came from the leaky faucet in the bathroom sink. The super of our building, Dominic, had promised to fix it, along with the stove, the oven, the pipes that ran through the walls in the living room, the knocking heater, and the refrigerator that oozed brown water. Dominic evidently looked at our kitchen the way missionaries look at Hollywood Boulevard or aid workers look at Calcutta. There was so much to do, it was too overwhelming to even start the job.

Dominic had also promised to fix my bathroom door. Mom had her bedroom on the other side, and we shared the bathroom. But my door had begun to rot, and Dominic made this problem even worse by halfway fixing it. He took down the door and never got around to replacing it, so the dripping water bothered me much more now that I couldn't shut the door. Mom hung up one of my old Barbie sheets across the doorway in the meantime. I used to sleep under those sheets when I was five years old. Dozens of princess Barbies danced on the borders. Identical Barbies in identical pink dresses, their faces plastered with big smiles, their eyes looking completely vacant. Now they kind of reminded me of some of the girls at my school.

I rolled out of bed and rubbed my eyes as I stumbled into the bathroom. The water was dripping steadily – drip, drip, drip. I turned on the hot water – which meant warm water on a good day – and washed my face.

It wasn't a bad face, I thought as I looked in the mirror. It was a good face in bad circumstances. Okay, so maybe I didn't look as 'L.A.' as some of the other girls at Rosewood, but they had three-hundred-dollar highlights and M·A·C lip glosses working in their favour. I had Bonne Belle Lip Smackers and haircuts courtesy of my mom and her kitchen scissors. It wasn't like I was jealous or anything. In fact, I kind of felt sorry for those girls – they had to spend all that extra time getting ready in the morning, whereas I was free to spend my time . . . listening to the water drip in the sink.

I felt something soft brush my ankle and looked down to see Desperate. Desperate was the name I gave my cat when I discovered her as a kitten, shivering on a side street that ran between Pacific Avenue and the Venice canals. Desperate had been just a placeholder name until I could think of something else, but as I got to know her, I saw that Desperate fit her name, the same way I fit mine. Desperate had grown up healthy, but she had really uncontrollable fur that stuck out all over the place. Bad fur days, they call it. Desperate was a good friend. She clawed on the furniture and chewed up the hats Mom made, but she always looked sorry and would make up for it by clawing on the sheet across the bathroom door until she made fringe out of the Barbies that ran across the bottom.

'Meow,' said Desperate, which could have meant anything from 'I want food,' to 'There is a mouse in the kitchen that just a few minutes ago was alive and well. I cannot control these violent tendencies. I must be stopped.'

'Did you get another mouse?' I asked Desperate.

'Meow,' she replied. A confession? We would soon see.

On the way to the kitchen I passed by Mom's bedroom. The door was halfway open, so I peeked inside. She was fast asleep, her pink-and-white waitress uniform hung across a wing-back chair. According to restaurant regulation she had to wear three-inch heels and a high ponytail along with the frilly uniform, like a cartoon waitress come to life. She waited tables at the End Zone, a sports bar on Ocean Avenue. It was the regular hangout for a bunch of San Diego Chargers fans, and every time a game came on, the fans would crowd the bar and watch it on one of the giant screens, whooping and screaming when the Chargers won, falling silent and forgetting to tip if they lost. Needless to say, my mom was not particularly fond of the Chargers or football teams in general. They reminded her of drunken men and stale beer and overcooked chicken wings. Of a life spent toiling away at some menial job, when it should have been spent running her own hat empire.

Back when she was in her mid-twenties, my mom had a brief but very successful hat-making career. She was studying fashion design at UCLA when a boutique owner saw a hat she'd made and asked my mom to make a bunch more. Eventually Mom dropped out of school to pursue fame and fortune as a famous headwear designer. Everything should have been perfect, but then she met a doctoral student in behavioural psychology who got her pregnant and abandoned her. I'd never met him, but I looked him up on the computers at school. Apparently he lived in Beverly Hills now and had a flourishing practice in adolescent and teen psychotherapy. Sometimes I liked to imagine what he'd say if I made an appointment and showed up in his office wanting to discuss my 'abandonment issues'.

Anyway, Mom had to go to work to support me, and her hat creations kind of fell by the wayside. She kept it up as much as she could, making hats from random scraps she got out of the remnants bin at Material Girl and selling them on commission out of a little shop on Abbot Kinney. Every so often I'd spot someone on the street wearing one of Mom's designs, which was always sort of cool. I'd tried to tell her to jack up the price; that's what really makes designers take off. Look at Kate Spade, I told her. But Mom just wouldn't do it. Maybe she was afraid that no one would buy the hats at all then, and what little extra money they made would just disappear.

Don't get me wrong – we weren't completely miserable, and we certainly didn't spend our time sitting around feeling sorry for ourselves. Okay, so we didn't have a ton of extra cash to throw around, but I never went hungry or anything like that. And besides, we had a lot of fun together, Mom and I.

The morning sunlight came in and lit up Mom's face.

Despite the fact that she joked about being my 'silly-looking old mother', I thought she was beautiful. She had glossy brown hair and smooth, clear skin. The men at the sports bar hit on her all the time, and some of them were kind of gross about it when they'd had a few too many Amstel Lights. One night Mom came home with buffalo wing sauce in the shape of a handprint on the back of her dress. I asked her about it and she said, 'Some drunk guy tried to grab me, so I shoved my knee right in his fifty-yard line. He spent the next ten minutes having a time-out.' And then she'd laughed her warm, coppery laugh, and I'd laughed, too, and before we knew it, we were clutching our stomachs and the tears were running down our faces.

I guess you could say Mom's pretty much my best friend – my best friend who just happens to be a lot older and kind of looks like me.

Most mornings she woke up in time to have breakfast with me, but at the moment she looked so peaceful I didn't want to wake her. I went to the kitchen and made breakfast while Desperate watched me like a hawk, even though her food bowl was full. Desperate always wanted what other people had, which made L.A. the perfect place for her.

When I finished eating breakfast, I packed lunch and headed out. I cringed when I noticed that yet another let-ter was taped to our door. At least I'd seen it before my mom. It was almost becoming a reflex – ripping off the note and sticking it in my pocket.

I found my slightly rusty blue ten-speed chained to the stairway of our apartment complex, put my backpack in the basket, and started down our street, which ran through the heart of Venice, a funky little area in the south-western part of Los Angeles. Venice used to be full of artists and gangs – but more and more young professionals were moving in, fixing up the places and driving up property values – and rent. Our street wasn't as nice as the ones that ran through the canals, or even the area around the vintage shops on Abbot Kinney. But on the other hand, it wasn't as bad as the Oakwood area, where someone was always holding someone up at gunpoint.

Most of the girls who attended school at Rosewood were from Beverly Hills, Malibu, or Bel Aire, and they had parents who gave them BMWs and Mercedeses to drive to school. I didn't even have a Pinto. And since the bus service would have cost a lot of money (Rosewood was a private school – it was expensive just to *breathe* there), I was forced to ride my bike, enduring whistles and catcalls every morning as I rode down Washington Boulevard. But that was okay with me. As a result of my enforced transportation, I would have a better-developed character and sleeker legs than my classmates.

Every so often when I was in a bad mood, I'd feel a tiny bit sorry for myself, but then I'd snap back to reality and put all my energies into making straight 'A's so that some-day I'd get into a good college on scholarship, the same way I'd earned my full ride at Rosewood. Then I'd be the one laughing from the dorm room of Brown or Duke while those other girls . . . well, married doctors and lived in bigger houses in Beverly Hills. But still, they would have bad character development and by then their legs would probably be really fat.

When I arrived at school, a few of the girls were hanging

out on the marble staircase that led up to the big double doors of Rosewood Academy. The weather had cooled a little – strange for September – and three of them were wearing cream turtleneck sweaters. I wondered if they'd planned it the night before.

While I chained my bicycle to the iron rails of the staircase, I overheard one of the girls, Bridget Walsh, squealing about something.

'Wait, really? I can't believe it. Seriously?'

Bridget Walsh's father was a big Hollywood producer. He'd put Bridget in a Disney movie when she was six years old, and she'd been wanting to act ever since. She always seemed to be practising for an audition, but she never got any parts. Maybe today she was trying out to be Perky, the little-known eighth Dwarf.

'This is just so totally exciting,' Mary Robbins agreed. 'Definitely the new M.F.' Mary was really into calling things 'the new M.F.' M.F. stood for Most Fabulous. Previously the title of 'new M.F.' had been bestowed upon her favourite strappy sandals, the new season of *The Real World*, and Crest Whitestrips.

'This really is amazing,' Sally Phillips said, nodding. 'I can't believe royalty is coming to Rosewood.' Usually their conversations didn't interest me that much, but this actually sounded kind of cool.

'Royalty like Michael Jackson, the King of Pop?' I asked, smirking. Bridget looked at me blankly, blinked, and shook her head. Most of the girls at school didn't really get my sense of humour.

'Huh? Nooo. Like, real royalty.' She held up a copy of

the newspaper and waved it in front of me. 'As in Princess Carina from Vineland.'

'Oh,' I said.

'This is totally going to bring such good publicity to our school,' Darcy Carroll said, flipping her hair.

'Totally,' said Stacy Lomax. 'Definitely good publicity.'

'Why is she coming here?' I asked. 'I mean, to what do we owe this great honour?' I added, holding back a grin.

'I heard her grandmother went to Rosewood in the forties,' said Bridget, 'and so it's kind of a PR event. You know, royal granddaughter returns after sixty years.'

'I wonder if that means they're going to donate something fabulous to the school,' Mary said. 'They are completely loaded, like Bill Gates loaded.'

'Cool,' said Darcy. 'Maybe they'll get Anna Sui to design the new school uniform or get a spa put in the locker rooms.'

I scowled, remembering my own need for a serious donation. Turning away from the group, I opened up my backpack and took out the letter I had found taped to the door. While the other girls continued to giggle and squeal and overuse the word *totally*, I scanned the message.

Dear Tenant,

As you know, I have raised the price of your rent by $200, well within my rights as a landlord, as this is not a rent-controlled property. Due to the unfortunate passing away of my mother, I am now the sole owner of the apartment complex. As a result, I have changed her very lax rules on late payments. You have not yet paid your August rent in full, and it's already mid-September.

> This is your third notice. Please remit payment to the
> building superintendent, Dominic Rocco, immediately.
> Failure to act in a timely manner will result in more seri-
> ous measures.

I folded the letter back up, my pulse racing. This was the worst one yet. *More serious measures* – what did that mean? I shoved the letter into my backpack. We'd have the money soon, if the Chargers could just get themselves together and win a couple of games. I didn't want my mom to freak out in the meantime. What was the point, when there was nothing we could do?

'Princess Carina has the best clothes!' Mary sighed. 'I wonder if she has a personal stylist or if she picks them out herself.'

'You know, you kind of look like her, Julia,' Sally said, chewing on a silver-lacquered thumbnail.

I raised my eyebrows. 'Right,' I said. 'I think maybe you put in the wrong prescription contacts today.'

The others all looked at me closer, glancing back and forth between me and the picture in the newspaper. 'That's so weird,' Bridget said. 'Julia, you actually do look like her. I mean, if you plucked your eyebrows and did something with your hair . . .'

I shook my head, letting out a laugh. Me and the princess of Vineland, long lost twins. That was a good one. If only plucking some eyebrows and getting a haircut *could* turn me into a princess. I had a feeling Princess Carina didn't have to hide scary landlord letters from her queen mother.

'I hear the princess gets her highlights from some special stylist who flies in from Milan,' Mary said. 'Apparently he uses some revolutionary technique that only two other people in the world know how to do. I really want to see her up close and ask her about it.'

'I don't think you're going to get a chance,' Bridget said. 'There's just going to be an assembly where she makes a few statements about what Rosewood meant to her grandmother, and then they're going to do a quick tour, and then she's out of here.'

Gwendolyn Jones came bouncing up. She was the head reporter for the *Rosewood Weekly*, and her specialty was breaking news that everyone knew about already. None of the students ever gave her quotes, so she relied on the teachers, who liked her because she always raised her hand and vehemently agreed with anything they said.

She stuck a paper in my hands, and then she was off.

I glanced down at the headline: PRINCESS COMES TO ROSEWOOD! GET A HOME EC TEACHER'S PERSPECTIVE IN AN EXCLUSIVE INTERVIEW!

I let the paper drop and went inside. It looked like I was the only person at Rosewood who couldn't care less about the princess of Vineland coming to our school, probably because I was also the only one there who had more important things to worry about. Things Princess Carina couldn't help with, no matter how well plucked her eyebrows were.

Chapter 3

I had never been so bored in my entire life. And for someone who has been forced to sit through countless state dinners and fatherly lectures, that was saying a lot. Not to mention my daily history lessons with Master Heinrich the Lisper. He'd been known to stop midsentence and stare off into nowhere for as long as five minutes at a time before coming back to an entirely different thought.

Honestly. I'd clocked him.

He reminded me of that teacher at the beginning of *Ferris Bueller's Day Off*, one of my favourite American classics. After I first saw it, I always used to daydream about what I would do if I got a day off from being a princess. Naturally these daydreams would most often occur right in the middle of one of Heinrich the Lisper's dazes.

'Okay, this is torture,' Ingrid groaned, slumping in the plastic chair next to mine. I was sitting up so straight, she looked like she was a full foot shorter than me with that posture. 'How long does it take to prep a plane?' she demanded. 'You put in the gas, you restock the alcohol, and you're done.'

'Ooh! They have alcohol?' I asked loudly, just to irritate Fröken Killroy.

'Girls, please,' Fröken Killroy said, her fingers folded primly in her lap. 'We are in a public place.'

'Could have fooled me,' I said under my breath. We were, in fact, sitting in the middle of Vineland International Airport, waiting for the airline people to gas up our charter flight to the United States, but the security detail was making every other traveller in the place take a fifty-yard detour around our gate. There didn't seem to be another living soul for miles. It was kind of like being at the palace. My bubble was following me everywhere.

'Come on,' Ingrid said, standing up and grabbing my hand. 'We need reading material.'

I was barely out of my seat when Fröken Killroy stood up. 'Oh no. You are not going to that newsstand. The men have not done a security sweep,' she said. 'If you wanted something to read, you should have brought it from home.'

'Do you really think some gum peddler is waiting in there to assassinate the princess?' Ingrid asked sarcastically. She was so not helping the situation.

'Five minutes, Fröken,' I said, raising my eyebrows at her. 'Please?'

'Carina, your parents have entrusted me with your safety,' she began, her wattle quivering beneath her chin. It was so ick I had to look away.

'Exactly!' Ingrid put in. 'And if she doesn't get something to read soon, she's going to start . . . losing brain cells! You wouldn't want that to happen, now, would you?'

With that, Ingrid started to pull me away towards the

little news-and-candy shop (not that I struggled). I cast a fake helpless look back at Killjoy and she flattened her mouth into a line before calling out, 'Five minutes!'

The newsstand was brightly lit and the glossy, colourful magazine covers beckoned my name, but even the sight of the new French *Vogue* couldn't pull the frown off my face. We hadn't even left the country yet and already my excitement was starting to die a slow death. This trip was going to be zero fun with Fröken Killroy breathing down my neck.

'She's even worse than usual,' I said as Ingrid started to grab handfuls of chocolate bars and gum. 'It's like being my sole chaperone has got her drunk with power.'

'I know. I'm surprised she hasn't fitted you for a leash yet,' Ingrid said, tossing a pack of Bubblelicious back into the bin.

'Don't say that in front of her,' I warned. 'It'll give her ideas.'

'Cheer up, C.! We are going to find a way to get you to that concert or my name isn't . . . ooh! Leo!'

She rushed across the tiny shop and snatched a new copy of *People* magazine from a rack. We both hovered over it, salivating at the new pictures of Leonardo DiCaprio. I swear, those few Leoless years after *Titanic* were just sad. He was my first official crush, and although Shane West had helped me through the dry spell, a million viewings of *A Walk to Remember* could never replace a good Leo fix.

'Thank God he made a comeback,' Ingrid said, flipping the pages with her thumb. 'Ugh! Look! There he is with his model brigade.' She scrunched her nose as she checked out the all-leg girls surrounding Leo at some party in L.A.

L.A. Soon we were going to be there. It was going to stop being this almost mythical place that only existed on DVDs and in *InStyle* and become an actual city with me in it!

'You know, you should totally throw a party at the palace and invite him,' Ingrid said, blowing a gum bubble. Ingrid chews gum like a fiend when we're in non-smoking public areas. 'I bet he'd love to party with a royal.'

'Please,' I replied, tossing my hair over my shoulder. 'My parents' idea of a wild bash was that croquet party they threw for Grandmama's seventieth. It was more yawn fest than L.A. chic.'

Ingrid looked up from the magazine for the first time. 'Those two must learn to use their power for good instead of evil.'

I laughed and walked along the wall of magazines, picking up an *Elle*, a *W*, and a *Seventeen* with Avril Lavigne on the cover. I wondered what my parents would do if I sent out invitations to a party without asking them. I couldn't even imagine the fit my father would throw. Maybe that dungeon he was always idly threatening me with would turn out to be real. I looked down at Avril's heavily lined, defiant eyes and sighed. She would throw an unsanctioned party if she were a princess. Then again, if she'd been born a princess, she probably would have run away before her sixth birthday.

'Oh my God! Carina! You are *not* going to believe this,' Ingrid said, sauntering over to me. She held out the *People* in front of my face. 'Check out the shot on the right.'

'So?' I said. It was yet another in a seemingly endless

stream of grainy photographs of Prince William playing polo. He was swinging his club and had his head tipped back in a laugh, flashing his perfect teeth. I ran my tongue over my own teeth out of habit. My braces had just been taken off a few weeks ago and I now had my own perfectly photoworthy smile, but I was still paranoid that they were all going to move back to their formerly crooked state.

'Not Willy,' Ingrid said. 'Look at the horse behind his.'

I glanced right and felt my stomach drop. Sitting astride a beautiful white horse was none other than Markus Ingvaldsson. I couldn't believe it. Markus was playing polo with Prince William now? Would it never end? I could just imagine the details I was going to be subjected to when I saw him again.

'William has a good shot, but he was no match for me,' I heard Markus brag in my head. Of course, Markus would never actually *say* something so blatantly egotistical, but I knew he thought he was the greatest thing since beluga caviar.

Unfortunately, my father was in agreement with that assessment. Just wait until he found out that Markus was now hobnobbing with England's elite. He'd probably call me right away to make sure that I knew and that I'd ask Markus about it at the embassy ball. My dad hadn't even bothered to call me to wish me a safe trip, but he would *definitely* call me about this.

'I can't believe he got to play with Prince William,' Ingrid said.

'Well, he is the god of polo,' I replied sarcastically. 'I think he was born with a polo stick in his hand.'

'More like up his butt,' Ingrid replied.

I laughed and pushed the magazine and her hands away. 'That whole mag just went down an entire notch.'

'No problem,' Ingrid said. She laid the magazine down flat on top of a stack of newspapers and tore the page with the Markus and Willy picture out. Then she folded it up and stuffed it into her bag. 'Leo is now untainted,' she said, executing a little bow.

'Thanks, Ingrid,' I said as she handed me the magazine. I put it on top of my stack and headed for the register, hoping the woman behind the counter wouldn't recognise me. If she did, she'd probably insist I take the stuff for free, just like every other shopkeeper in the world. Just once it would be cool to pay for something like a normal person.

'Uh . . . *scusi*. You are the princess of Vineland, yes?'

I turned around to find the single hottest guy I had ever seen in my life standing in front of me. He had curly brown hair with obviously natural blond highlights and was wearing a kind of ragged T-shirt and jeans. The backpack slung over his shoulder was decorated with all kinds of colourful patches and was all tattered and stained. Just imagining the places that backpack had been made me ache to get on that plane.

But not before I found out who this piece of perfection was.

'*Si*,' I replied with a flirtatious smile. '*Come stai?*'

So glad I absorbed the little Italian I had. His whole handsome face lit up.

'*Bene! Grazie!*' he replied. Then he held out a pad and a pen with shaking hands. 'Please may I have your autograph?' he asked.

Ingrid slid up next to me and her eyes widened. 'You bet your ravioli you can,' she said under her breath, causing me to snort a laugh. Very unprincesslike.

I was just reaching out for the pen and pad when Fröken Killroy descended upon us like a testosterone-seeking missile.

'I'm sorry, but the princess has no time for autographs,' she said, grabbing me by the shoulders and turning me away from one stunned Italian. I felt my cheeks flush red with humiliation. How could she do that to me in front of him? He was clearly a man of the world, and here I was being protected by a nanny!

I whirled away from her and grabbed the pen out of the guy's hand. 'Nonsense, Fröken,' I said through my teeth. 'My father, the *king*, has told me to always make time for the international visitors to our great nation.'

Killroy narrowed her eyes at me. She knew the game I was playing, pulling out the king card, but it worked anyway. She stepped back while I signed the autograph.

'*Arrivederci!*' I called after the traveller after he thanked me a couple dozen times. Then I turned around and dropped my stack of magazines on the counter.

'Oh no,' Killroy said, grabbing the *People*. 'This rag is not fit reading for a princess. What if someone were to see you?'

'You can't tell me what to read,' I said weakly. There wasn't much fight left in me after the autograph incident. Killroy had a way of wearing me down. Maybe it was the pinched quality of her voice. The high-wave frequency was zapping away my energy stores.

'Carina, your parents left you in my care,' she said for the billionth time that day. 'And I am *going* to take care of you.'

She was about to slap the *People* down on the rack again, but Ingrid intercepted it.

'Well, you can't tell *me* what to read,' she said snottily. We both grinned at Killroy in triumph. Sometimes it was so good to have a friend like Ingrid.

'Fine,' Killroy said huffily. 'I want you two back at the gate in one minute.' Then she turned and marched off, her brand-new silk travelling suit swishing as she went.

Ingrid placed the *People* down on the counter along with a copy of *Us Weekly* and *Inside,* Vincland's very own gossip magazine – the one that was constantly printing unauthorised photos of me and always seemed to get me on days when my hair wouldn't defrizz or my skin was rebelling. They'd even managed to get a shot of me when I still had the metal plate taped to my face after my nose job. Of course, that one had never been printed. My mother and father had been tipped off about it and had somehow prevented the photo from hitting the stands. I always thought they were making a big deal out of nothing. After all, it wasn't like people weren't going to notice the fact that the monster bump had somehow disappeared from my nose. But that was my parents for you – more concerned with appearances than anything else. They had been too busy to pick me up from the hospital after the operation, but they hadn't been too busy to bribe some journalist into early retirement.

'What are we going to do about Killjoy?' I asked as the lady at the register punched at the keys.

'That woman *needs* a boyfriend,' Ingrid said, whipping

out some cash and paying for her magazines.

'Ew! Ingrid!' I said, sticking out my tongue as I fished in my bag for my wallet. 'Thanks. Now I have a mental picture of Killroy kissing some guy burned into my memory for ever.'

'Well, I don't know how we're going to shake her when we get to L.A., but I'm going to get you to that concert, Carina, I promise.'

I smiled my thanks but didn't get a chance to answer. The woman behind the counter was dry heaving as she gaped at me, and it was more than a little distracting.

'Carina? Carina! You *are* Princess Carina!' she cried. 'Please, take the magazines. You must not pay!'

I took a deep breath. Guess my wallet was staying right where it was. 'Thank you,' I said to the woman as I slid the magazines off the counter. I knew better than to protest. I'd stopped doing that somewhere around age thirteen when a man at the Burberry shop had got so indignant at my insistence to pay, he had walked off the job.

Soon you will be in L.A., where there's a movie star on every corner, I told myself as Ingrid and I took our sweet time walking back to the gate. *In L.A. you'll be just another famous face.*

In L.A. my fondest dream would come true. I'd be just like everyone else.

Chapter 4

'There's nothing,' I said, rustling the newspaper in front of me as I walked. The page was covered with red circles and 'X's over jobs I'd considered applying for and then decided against. They either demanded too much time, paid too little money, or required experience. Unless I could somehow fake working knowledge of a meat slicer, a jackhammer, or a boom mike, I was out of luck. 'In the entire city of Los Angeles, there is not one job I can do.'

'That's not true,' my friend Elizabeth protested, folding her half of the want ads over her hand. She pulled her lollipop out of her mouth and held up the newspaper for me to see. 'Look! There are like fifty ads for nude models.'

I rolled my eyes and hip-checked Liz as we walked along the path on the beach, heading for the Santa Monica pier. Elizabeth was a photographer (an artist, unlike paparazzi-bound Gwendolyn Jones), and for the past couple of weeks she'd been working on a project for her art class called 'Wacky L.A.' She'd been hitting all the big tourist spots, taking secret photos of unsuspecting day-trippers and vacationers. Today she wanted to catch people on the Tilt-A-Whirl with their about-to-barf faces on.

'You'll find something. Don't worry,' Elizabeth told me as we climbed the stairs to the pier.

I sighed, wishing I could be as optimistic. I knew Elizabeth was just trying to help, but the fact that she was joking around only proved that she didn't get the direness of the situation. Her dad was some big movie mogul guy, constantly making deals on his cell phone and buying cars for his kids whenever some romantic comedy opened well. Elizabeth was a good friend, and one of very few unshallow people at school, but until she knew what it was like to deflect angry phone calls from the landlord so that her mom could get some extra sleep . . . well, there was no way she could really understand.

'Ooh! What about a dog walker?' Elizabeth suggested, tucking her long red bangs behind her ear. She had the short-in-back, long-in-front Kelly Osborne haircut and the goth-punk wardrobe to go with it. Her many silver rings glittered in the sunlight, and I noticed her purple nail polish was severely chipping. It also pretty much matched the colour her tongue and lips were stained from the lollipop. 'You'd be outside . . . getting exercise . . .'

'Please. All dogs hate me. You know this,' I told her. 'It's like they can sense I'm a cat person.'

I folded up the newspaper and stuffed it into my back-pack. I'd look the ads over again later. There had to be something in there – some way I could earn some money to help my mother out with the back rent. But for now, it was time for Elizabeth to pay up. She'd bribed me into coming along with her by promising to buy us a ride on the Ferris wheel.

'You ready for this?' I asked, rubbing my hands together as I looked up at the ride looming over the Pacific.

Elizabeth gulped. 'Did I mention I was afraid of heights?'

'Come on! I bet you can get some killer shots from up there. It'll be the next M.F.!' I said, imitating Bridget's affected voice.

'I'll go if you promise never to use that abbreviation again,' Elizabeth said, levelling me with a glare.

'Deal.'

As I was walking towards the Ferris wheel, I tripped over a warped board and Elizabeth reached up to grab my arm. It was like a reflex for her. Let's just say it wasn't the first time I'd tripped myself in Elizabeth's presence. It wasn't the first time I'd tripped myself that *day*.

We climbed onto the Ferris wheel, and as we ascended towards the perfect blue sky, Elizabeth's knuckles turned white, her hands clutching the safety rail.

'Deep breaths,' I told her. 'You'll be fine.'

We stopped at the very top and I followed my own advice, breathing slowly and telling myself to chill. Everything was going to be fine. If I could just win the lottery.

'Wow. It really is beautiful up here,' Elizabeth said. She pulled out her camera and snapped a few shots.

'What's wrong?' she asked, turning to me suddenly.

'What do you mean?'

'You keep sighing,' Elizabeth said.

I hadn't even realised it. I looked down at my hands

and bit my lip. 'Liz, you ever wish you could . . . like . . . I don't know, be someone else for a while?'

'All the time,' Elizabeth said, with a 'duh' face. 'Gwen Stefani. Hands down. The day she married Gavin Rossdale. Although I don't know if I would have gone with the pink on the gown.'

I laughed and settled back, looking off across the water. 'I would just like to know what it's like to not have to worry about money. Even if it was just for a day. I'm so sick of stressing.'

Elizabeth leaned back and wrapped her arm around my shoulders, resting her head against mine. 'You'll figure it out, Jules. You always do.'

That's exactly the problem, I thought. *I'm sixteen years old. I shouldn't* have *to figure it out.*

My heart felt heavy enough to drop into the water below. I couldn't believe I was thinking this way. Since when was I such a whiner? But the self-pity train was off and running and, for the moment, there was nothing I could do to stop it.

I bet Princess Carina never has to worry about money, I thought. *I bet whatever she wears to school tomorrow could pay our rent for the rest of the year. Maybe I could just steal her clothes. She'll probably have a servant standing by with an extra set anyway.*

I took a deep breath as the Ferris wheel cart slowly descended to earth. Maybe I would skip school the next day. Because suddenly I wasn't sure I was going to be able to sit through the little royal assembly without jumping up and strangling Princess I Have Everything.

Chapter 5

The morning that Princess Carina was expected to grace us with her royal presence, it was like everyone I knew had turned into a giggling ball of mush. Every class I went to, people were whispering, passing around pictures of Carina they'd downloaded from the Internet, and giggling over a clipping of some guy she was apparently dating. By the time we got to the auditorium that afternoon, I was definitely over it.

Well, actually, I had never been under it, whatever 'it' was. This girl knew nothing about us, cared nothing about us, and was basically going to waste thirty minutes of our time just so everyone could drool all over her.

'You are sooo gonna love me,' Elizabeth said as she approached the aisle seat I'd saved for her. She raised her eyebrows and pulled two grande cups of Starbucks coffee out from behind her back. 'Energy boost for your interview this afternoon.'

'You are a goddess,' I told her, reaching out for my cup carefully as Elizabeth sat down next to me.

I clasped the paper cup with both hands, holding it

away from me and my responsible-looking outfit. I had never had a cup of coffee without getting at least one drop on myself, but I definitely needed the caffeine. I had barely slept at all last night, stressing about the job interview I'd lined up for this afternoon.

Yesterday after leaving the pier I'd finally found one job I could potentially do – filing at a nearby lighting supply company called Take Five Lighting – and when I'd called, they'd asked me to come in today. Now I was wearing my only good black skirt and an old but still workable silk blouse of my mom's, and if I got anything on it, I was done for. There were no other options in my closet.

'So where the heck is this princess chick anyway?' Elizabeth asked, slurping on her coffee. A few drops fell onto the front of her denim jacket and I winced, but Liz didn't even notice. 'I mean, shouldn't arriving on time be, like, part of her royal programming?'

'Nah. She probably figures she's so important we can all just wait for her,' I replied, taking a quick sip.

The auditorium seemed even louder than it did before our usual assemblies as everyone anticipated what the princess would be wearing and whether or not she'd show us her tiara. Gwendolyn Jones was running around the room, pausing every few feet to aim her camera at the stage, looking for the perfect angle. Darcy, who sat a few rows up, kept whipping her head around every two seconds to see whether the girl had arrived yet. Just watching her was giving me whiplash.

Finally Headmistress Weathers took the stage, her low heels click-clacking as she walked over to the

48

podium. An instant hush fell over the room and the air actually sizzled. This was so pathetic. Rosewood was a pretty exclusive school, and important people were always coming in to speak. But when Maya Angelou had visited last year to read some of her Pulitzer Prize-winning poetry, half the girls in school had sat back and done their nails.

'Ladies of Rosewood Academy, may I have your undivided attention, please?' Weathers said, gripping both sides of the podium with her bony fingers. Elizabeth mouthed the headmistress's opening perfectly. She always said the exact same thing whenever she stood up in front of the school, whether she was introducing a guest or announcing a change in the lunch menu.

'As you all know, we have a very important visitor with us this afternoon,' Weathers said, her dull brown eyes actually displaying a little spark of something. Maybe pride at having landed us such an illustrious speaker as the born-into-greatness princess of Vineland.

A little wave of excited whispers crossed the room and Weathers waited for complete silence before continuing.

'I'm sure, thanks to our intrepid reporter, Gwendolyn Jones, you all are aware that Princess Carina's grandmother attended this very school back in the 1940s.'

Weathers shot an appreciative little glance in Gwendolyn's direction and Gwendolyn, of course, flushed with pride.

'Suck-up,' Liz and I both said under our breath.

'Now, not only has Princess Carina of Vineland done us the honour of including our academy as one of her stops on her goodwill tour, but Rosewood is, in fact, her *first* official stop here in the United States,' Ms Weathers announced, lifting her chin triumphantly. Everyone burst into applause. Elizabeth and I exchanged a look.

'Yeah, cuz she wanted to get it over with,' Elizabeth said, shifting in her seat.

'It is incumbent upon us to make sure that Princess Carina receives a welcome to our country that is worthy of a royal figure such as herself,' Ms Weathers continued. 'And a welcome worthy of the granddaughter of one of our most accomplished graduates.'

As Weathers started to instruct us on the proper welcome (it seemed a standing ovation was in order), Gwendolyn began to strut around the room again, snapping photos of the headmistress from every conceivable angle. I had a feeling that the next issue of the *Rosewood Reporter* was going to be a fat one.

'And now, without further ado, I present to you Her Royal Highness, Princess Carina of Vineland!'

Every girl in the room jumped to her feet, and the applause was deafening. I sighed, looked at Elizabeth, and dragged myself up slowly so as not to spill my coffee. I could sort of see the figure of a girl walking across the stage, but I couldn't get a good look at her because the freshmen in front of me were climbing up on the seats of their chairs for a better view. The standing ovation continued for at least five minutes, and I could see the flash of Gwendolyn's camera going off over and over again. Liz and I were the first to sit back down.

'Thank you, thank you so much,' the princess said into the microphone when everyone finally calmed down.

The girls in front of me stifled their squeals and settled into their seats, and I got my first look at fabulousness.

It wasn't exactly a life-altering moment. Princess Carina was pretty, yeah, but not any prettier than anyone else who went to this school. She was wearing a plain, slim, sleeveless dress, and her long blonde hair hung straight over her shoulders. About the only thing that set her apart from the students in the audience was her presence. I had to admit she was more relaxed and poised up there than I would have been if faced with hundreds of people. But then, she probably did this every day. I wondered how she would react if she were faced with one of the dead mice I had to scoop up every other morning.

'I want to thank Headmistress Weathers for that incredible welcome,' she said, turning her head to smile at the faculty section to the left of the stage. When she did, one of the spotlights caught her earring and there was a sharp flash of light.

'Holy crap. You see the size of those things?' Elizabeth said under her breath, earning a scowl from one of the frosh in front of us.

Okay, so that was something else that set her apart. Forget her clothes – one *earring* could pay my rent for a year and probably send me to college for four.

I looked down at my responsible hire-me outfit and told myself not to compare apples and oranges, but faced with a spectacle like this one, it was nearly impossible. Here I was stressing over an interview for a seven-dollar-an-hour job, and there was a person in this room who could probably bail my mom out of all her money issues without even missing the cash.

Sometimes life seriously sucked.

'Growing up in Vineland, my grandmother would always tell me amazing stories about her time here in Los Angeles and at Rosewood Academy,' Carina began, somehow seeming to make eye contact with every last person in the room. She didn't even blink or stutter when Gwen got right in her face with her blinding flashbulb. 'You may not believe that a girl who spent her childhood in a castle would dream of being anywhere else, but I did. My grandmother loved her time here so much, cherished her friends and her education so deeply, that I couldn't help dreaming of one day coming to Rosewood and seeing it for myself. And now that I have, I can tell you it is everything I dreamed it would be.'

I rolled my eyes at Liz.

'Looking out at all of you, I can see what my grandmother loved so much – the sisterhood, the excitement of learning, the promise of the future,' Carina continued with a sickeningly sweet smile. 'Never forget that you *are* the future, *we* are the future. And I look forward to forming that future along with all of you.'

'I'm definitely gonna hurl,' I said.

'Thank you and God bless!' Carina finished, raising a hand in a wave.

The auditorium exploded with noise all over again and the girl sitting next to me jumped up, her elbow lifting my arm practically over my head . . . and dumping every last ounce of my grande coffee all over my shirt.

'No!' I screamed, completely drowned out by the cheering all around me.

'Oh God! Are you okay?' Elizabeth asked, standing up.

My eyes instantly filled with tears as I held my hands away from my soaked self. I could feel the warm liquid seeping through the fabric of my shirt, soaking my bra, and sticking to my skin.

I'm so dead, my brain recited over and over, images of me as responsible work girl flitting through my mind and right out the window. *I'm so dead I'm so dead I'm so dead.*

As Princess Carina continued to wave and bow and mouth her thank-yous to her adoring fans, I burst into frustrated tears and ran from the room.

Chapter 6

'You know, sometimes I cannot believe the ridiculous things those speechwriters make me say,' I blurted the second Ingrid and I were inside the sanctity of one of the ladies' rooms at Rosewood Academy. '"We are the future"? I mean, who says that?'

'You did,' Ingrid said, her eyes teasing.

'Thank you *so* much for your support,' I said.

'Oh, I was totally moved,' Ingrid joked.

I sighed and placed my purse on the dingy wooden countertop. I dug through it until I found my pressed powder and started to dab at my face. Why couldn't I just write my own speeches and say what *I* wanted to say? I was so sick of doing what everyone else expected me to do. And this was only one of many public appearances I was going to have to make while we were here. I already felt like I wanted to crawl out of my own skin.

'What is it, four thousand degrees in this place?' I said, sweat prickling under my arms and along my hairline. 'They could have at least turned on the air-conditioning for us.'

'Okay, C., you're being cranky even for you,' Ingrid said, leaning back against the wall. 'What's the problem?'

I took a deep breath and sighed again, dropping my make-up brush back into my bag. 'The problem is, this is the first five seconds we've had without Killjoy right on top of us, and we're only getting it because that Weathers person won't stop talking her ear off. This trip is going to be nothing like I expected. And do you know what I found out this morning? The embassy ball is the exact same night as the Toadmuffin concert. There's no way I can skip out on the ball.'

'Yeah, Killjoy will *definitely* notice that,' Ingrid said.

I felt myself descending towards tears and took another long breath. I would not go there. I had to remain calm. Once I started stressing, I would get all blotchy, and that mess on top of the sweating would paint a totally unpretty picture.

'I'm just going to have to accept it,' I told her, my stomach turning. 'There's no way I'm going to that concert.'

Ingrid exhaled a stream of smoke and looked at my reflection in the mirror. What I saw in her eyes made me want to cry even more. She didn't think it was possible, either. And once Ingrid started giving up, I knew I was really in trouble. It was so unfair. My first trip without my mother and I still wasn't going to get to do anything I wanted to do. Ribbit would be waiting for me all night long and he would never know how much I truly wanted to be there.

Sometimes life really sucked.

Suddenly there was a rustling of paper behind us and my heart hit my throat. I looked at the stall doors in the mirror, and one of them was closed. I'd never used a public bathroom before an official security sweep in my life. It hadn't even occurred to me that someone might be in the room with us.

Ingrid shot me a look, telling me not to move, and slowly crouched down to check under the doors.

'Um . . . hello? Don't you know eavesdropping on a royal conversation is a federal offence?' Ingrid said, smirking wickedly at me.

One of the doors swung open and out walked one of the sorriest-looking spectacles I'd ever seen – a girl of about my height with stringy brown hair, running mascara, and a huge brown stain on her blouse. She reminded me of Carrie at the end of that Stephen King movie after they've dumped the pig's blood on her. Okay, maybe not *that* bad, but still, it was the first image that came to mind.

'Well, I was just leaving,' the girl snapped, pulling in a noisy sniffle. She stuffed a wad of paper towels into the garbage can and glared at me. 'Sorry the temperature wasn't to your liking, Your *Highness*,' she said sarcastically as she swept past me.

For a split second I couldn't even find my voice. I was fairly certain that it was the first time anyone other than Ingrid had dared to insult me. I wasn't sure whether to hate the odd little urchin or respect her.

The girl started for the door, but Ingrid stepped in front of her, blocking her way.

'What's your name?' Ingrid asked, looking the girl up and down. I raised my eyebrows at Ingrid. She had that look on her face that meant she was having a brainstorm, but I couldn't imagine what she was thinking. Did she want to perform a charity makeover or something? I didn't think I had enough make-up in my bag for that.

'Excuse me,' the girl said flatly.

'Interesting name,' Ingrid said, scoffing a laugh. She stubbed out her cigarette on the top of the metal garbage can and smiled. 'You know, I think I am the premier criminal mastermind of the twenty-first century.'

'What are you talking about?' the girl asked. She turned to look at me. 'Who is this girl, your royal wacko?'

'I'm Ingrid,' my friend told her, reaching out to shake the girl's hand.

'Julia,' she replied, still watching us like we had just escaped from an asylum. Instead of touching Ingrid, she took a step or two back.

'Nice to meet you, Julia,' Ingrid said. 'And you've already met Her *Highness*, Carina.'

'Hello,' I said with a nod. Then I shot Ingrid a look. What was going on in that devious little mind of hers?

'You know, you two look a lot like each other,' Ingrid said, circling Julia, then me, her hand on her chin.

I had to work hard not to laugh. This girl was in serious need of a personal shopper. Not to mention a shower and some grooming lessons.

'I don't think so, Ingrid,' I said, zipping up my bag.

'I'm so outta here,' Julia said.

'Wait!' Ingrid said, stopping the girl in her tracks. 'Julia, just . . . humour me for a second. Come here and stand next to Carina.'

'Ingrid, where are you going with this?' I asked impatiently. 'I want to get out of here already.'

'You know the little problem we've been discussing non-stop since we left the palace?' Ingrid said, staring at me meaningfully. 'Well, we may have found the answer.'

I scrunched up my face in disbelief. How was this person going to help me rendezvous with the love of my life?

'I don't like the sound of that,' Julia said.

'Come on, you know you're curious,' Ingrid said. 'All I want you to do is stand next to her. She doesn't have royal cooties.'

Julia looked at me and sighed, then trudged over and stood to my left. We stared at each other in the mirror, her face annoyed, mine sceptical. Our eyes were a similar shape and colour and we were about the same height, but other than that . . .

'Okay, now, visualise with me, people,' Ingrid said, hovering next to Julia. 'Add more make-up, a few highlights, and some zit cream. Then all you'd have to do is lose the split ends, the slouch, and the unibrow, and voilà! You guys could be twins.'

Julia's face went white. 'Did you people travel all the way from Vineland just to randomly insult Americans?' she snapped.

'No, I—'

But Julia wasn't waiting around any longer. She pushed past Ingrid and flung open the heavy bathroom door so hard it smashed up against the wall. Now that little temper tantrum? *That* looked familiar.

'Wait!' Ingrid called out. 'I didn't mean it as an insult! I just meant that with a little work . . .'

She followed Julia out into the hallway and I looked at

my reflection and sighed. I still had no idea what Ingrid was thinking, but whatever it was, it was clear that Julia person was not going to be a willing participant. Which was fine with me. She had just a little too much attitude for my taste. And a little too little soap in her life, apparently.

Oh, well, at least I had a moment to myself to—

'Carina?' Fröken Killroy's voice split the silence like a bullet. She pushed into the bathroom and sniffed the air. 'Were you girls *smoking* in here?' Her mouth hung open in horror, causing her wattle to wiggle obscenely.

So much for my alone time.

Chapter 7

On the way home from school that afternoon, I pedalled so hard I thought my bike was going to shake apart. I'd had worse days – like the time I'd exploded a potato in the microwave, shorted out the whole building, and had angry people with souring milk yelling at my door in fifteen different languages – but this one was up there. I had planned on staying after school in the library and studying for my upcoming biology exam until it was time to leave for my interview. Now I had to get home, shower, find something to wear that looked semi-businesslike, and get myself down to the Take Five Lighting offices by five o'clock. All that and I had to look calm and poised and eager and happy when I got there.

Maybe I should have talked to Carina for a few minutes longer. She could have given me some tips.

But then again, *ugh!* Just thinking about those two girls made me pedal even *faster.* Where did they get off, picking on me like that? And they were such fakes! Carina didn't even believe a thing she'd said at that podium, and now the entire school was busy trying to remember it word for word because it was so *inspiring* to them.

If I never saw another princess again, I would die a happy girl.

'Julia! Hey, Julia!'

I slowed down a little bit, and my thighs burned from the sudden change in momentum. Without the wind from my speed I could feel the heat in my face as well. Who the hell had snapped me out of my adrenaline rush?

'Over here!'

I glanced across the street and saw none other than Ingrid herself, waving out the sunroof of a sleek black limo. Her whole torso was visible and she was grinning eagerly.

I rolled my eyes and started pedalling again. What was wrong with that girl? I wondered if the king and queen of Vineland knew their daughter was hanging out with a complete nutjob.

Suddenly I heard a screeching of tyres and a few angry horn honks. I skidded to a stop and almost fell over. The limo completed an illegal U-ey across four lanes of traffic and pulled up next to me. The door popped open and Ingrid leaned out, releasing a blast of cool air from inside the car.

'Come on, get in,' she said.

'Are you people crazy?' I blurted, trying to catch my breath. 'You could have been killed! Is your driver on crack?'

'Oh, B.B. does whatever we tell him to as long as the price is right,' Ingrid said, waving her hand.

I had to ask. 'B.B.?'

'Buyable Bill,' Ingrid said with a shrug. 'We're thinking about making him drive us to Vegas. Wanna come?'

She was definitely insane. 'Later,' I said, placing my feet on my pedals.

'Julia, seriously,' Ingrid said. 'We have a little proposition for you, and I think you'll find it very interesting.'

I stood there for a moment, studying her face. I had to admit, I was curious. What did the princess of Vineland and her wacky friend want with me?

'We'll give you a ride ho-ome . . . ,' Ingrid wheedled.

I looked up the street at the miles of hot road that lay ahead of me and realised that the mere breeze from the car had already chilled my ankles to a pleasant temperature. Plus I had never actually been in a limo before . . .

'All right,' I said finally, swinging my leg over my bike. 'But I have to go straight home.'

'Yes!' Ingrid cheered. 'B.B.! Put her bike in the back!'

A tall, square-jawed man stepped out of the driver's side and swiftly removed my bicycle from my grasp. As he toted it over to the huge trunk, I ducked into the limo and sank into the plush velvet seat. Carina sat across from me, her legs crossed at the ankle and her hands folded around her knee. Her panty hose shimmered as if they were made out of real silk. I crossed my ankles as well, to hide the stretched-out fabric of my tights that had gathered there in massive rolls.

Ingrid slammed the door and sat back next to me. 'Do you want to tell her or should I?' she asked Carina.

'I will,' Carina said, her eyes flicking over me as the driver returned to his place behind the wheel. The way she did it made me feel about one inch tall. 'But first, I'm hungry. Let's get something to eat. B.B.! I have a sushi craving.'

'I know just the place, miss,' B.B. said, starting up the engine. He picked up a cell phone and started to dial.

My stomach lurched as the limo pulled out into traffic. 'But I have to go home,' I said, glancing at my watch. 'I have a job interview at five.'

'Really? A working girl?' Ingrid said, giving me a fake-impressed frown. The girl had probably never worked on anything other than her abs. 'Don't worry. We'll get you there.'

Before I knew it, we were zipping up Wilshire Boulevard with some punk band I'd never heard before pounding through the speakers. Carina and Ingrid sang along with the lyrics, laughing as I stared out the window, feeling like I was being kidnapped. Hadn't these girls heard a word I'd said? I was in a time crunch here! But then, why would they bother listening to me? I was sure regular people were about as important to them as their royal nail clippings.

The limo pulled to a stop in front of Asakuma, an upscale sushi restaurant that Elizabeth's family ordered takeout from every Friday night. I'd been invited to a couple of their dinners and the food was amazing, but I'd never actually been in the restaurant before.

Ingrid and Carina climbed out of the limo the second B.B. opened the door, but I hesitated, looking down at my stained shirt.

'Oh! You can't go in there like that!' Carina said, causing my face to flush. 'B.B., open the trunk.'

The chauffeur did as he was told and I felt my jaw clench. The girl didn't even say please. How could anyone just take orders like that?

'Stay there a moment. We went shopping this morning,' Carina told me before disappearing behind the car. She came back with a light blue sweater and tossed it at me. 'Here. Wear this.'

I was about to protest when I felt the fabric beneath my fingers. It was the softest thing I'd ever touched. Cashmere. It had to be.

'I can't take—'

'Whatever,' Carina said. 'I bought two.'

The car door slammed, leaving me alone inside, and I checked the tag. Sure enough, the sweater was 100 per cent cashmere. And according to the still-attached price, it cost $500.

I stopped breathing. Her clothes really *could* pay the rent. My hands shaking, I unbuttoned the dirty blouse, folded it up, and put it in my bag, then pulled the soft sweater over my head. It was like wrapping myself up in a billion cotton balls. Only better. I tucked the price tag inside the neckline and stepped out of the car.

'Better already,' Ingrid said.

I glared at her.

'I mean, you look beautiful!' she corrected herself.

The moment we walked into the restaurant, a man in a suit stepped forward, all smiles, and held out his hand. 'Princess Carina, what an honour to meet you!' he said. Carina placed her hand in his and he grasped it for a moment. 'Your driver called ahead and requested a private room. I'm happy to say we can accommodate you. Just follow me.'

'Thank you,' Carina replied.

The man led us through a restaurant full of late lunchers in business suits and designer jeans. Cell phones rang, chopsticks clicked against dishes, and the conversation was hushed. He opened the door to a small room in the back corner, decorated with Japanese scrolls and puffy velvet pillows in maroons and purples. Carina slipped out of her shoes and sat down at the head of a table that rested on the floor. Ingrid and I did the same.

'Our friend is in a bit of a hurry, so we'll see the menu right away,' Carina told the maître d'. She looked at her glass, grimaced, and held it out to him. As far as I could tell, nothing was wrong with it. 'And I'll have a fresh glass,' she added dismissively. 'A clean one.'

'Of course,' the maître d' said. 'Please forgive me.'

Once again, no 'please' from Carina. My mother would have said this girl was raised in a barn, not a palace.

'Now, on to our little proposition,' Carina said, turning to me. 'This may be the only meal I get to eat away from my watchdog Fröken. Luckily that little school of yours needed her to deal with some legal paperwork. So if we're going to make a deal, it's got to be now.'

'Oooookay,' I said. What was she talking about, a deal? And what in the world was a watchdog fröken?

The waiter appeared with menus and placed three heaping plates of dumplings on the table. 'Appetisers with the chef's compliments,' he said. He placed a fresh glass of water next to Carina's plate and bowed before scurrying away.

Carina and Ingrid didn't even blink. They just started eating. All I could do was wonder why restaurants gave free food to people who could more than afford it when there were people who had to scrape together food stamps to keep themselves in mac and cheese.

'Have one,' Ingrid said.

'Not hungry, suddenly,' I replied. 'So what's this deal thing?' I asked. 'I kind of have someplace to be.'

Carina finished chewing, swallowed, sipped at her water, then spoke. 'I want you to impersonate me, just for one day, so that I can go to a concert. You know. Kind of like in that movie *Dave*?'

I had no clue what she was talking about.

'It was my idea,' Ingrid said proudly.

There was a moment of silence as I looked from Carina to Ingrid, then back again. Then I cracked up laughing.

'You guys *are* on something!' I said, reaching for my water.

'This is serious,' Carina said curtly. 'I *need* to go to this concert.'

'So go,' I said. 'Who's stopping you?' From what I'd seen so far, this girl could do pretty much whatever she wanted.

'Everyone! Everyone is stopping me!' she blurted, sounding like a toddler. I would have laughed if it wasn't so blatantly obvious that she was really upset.

'Listen, Julia,' Ingrid said. 'The Toadmuffin concert is this Saturday and Carina is supposed to meet a friend there, but her parents are insisting she go to this hospital that afternoon and then to an embassy ball that evening. All we want you to do is replace her for twenty-four hours.'

'Yeah, right,' I said with a laugh. 'Who put you up to this?'

'Nobody, I swear,' Ingrid said. 'We're dead serious.'

Okay. Now I was a little weirded out. What these girls were proposing was impossible, wasn't it? First of all, Carina and I might have had some tiny resemblance to each other, but there was no way I could *be* her. People would definitely notice the difference. And besides, I was a total klutz. I couldn't even get through one day without ruining my clothes. I had no idea what a person would *do* at an embassy ball, let alone what to wear or how to speak. And me on a dance floor? Not pretty. I'd be found out in five seconds.

'I think you guys have the wrong double,' I said, starting to get up from the table. My knees were like jelly. After all, the idea of playing princess for even a day was definitely butterfly-inducing. But it wasn't going to happen. I would make a fool out of myself if I tried. I made myself stand and grabbed my backpack. This wacky little plot was a little too wacky for my taste.

'We'll pay you,' Ingrid said loudly.

I stopped in my tracks. 'What makes you think I'll do it for money?' I asked.

'The fact that you stopped when I said it is kind of a tip-off,' Ingrid replied.

My body heat skyrocketed, but I turned to face her, swallowing my pride. 'When you say pay me, how much are you—'

'Ten thousand dollars,' Carina said bluntly. 'American cash.'

I sank back down to the floor. There was no way I could have continued to stand if I'd tried. Ten thousand dollars? Were they kidding? Did they have any idea what that kind of money could mean to me and my mother?

'Just think about it,' Ingrid said, leaning towards me. 'You get to be princess for a day. We'll give you a makeover and you'll get to wear all of Carina's clothes. *I* don't even get to do that!'

I barely heard what she was saying. *Ten thousand dollars. Ten thousand dollars. Ten thousand dollars.* The calculations were doing themselves in my mind. I could pay the rent for a whole year with that kind of money. My mother could cut back on her shifts. And I . . .

I was letting myself get sucked in by Princess Obnoxious and her sidekick, In-Your-Face Girl. Was I that easy of a mark? Was I so clearly . . . *needy* that they thought they could just buy me and make me do whatever they wanted?

Be Carina so the poor little rich girl can rebel against her parents.

I mean, I had my pride.

'I don't believe you,' I said, suddenly more than able to stand. 'Do you think that having money gives you the right to just make people do whatever you want?'

I turned to Carina and glared down at her. 'Poor little princess,' I said sarcastically as I gathered up my backpack again. 'You can have everything in the world and it's not enough. I feel so *bad* for you that you have to attend a *ball*. God! I am so outta here.'

I started to turn, but Ingrid grabbed my backpack and slipped a business card in the side pocket. 'In case you change your mind,' she said with a totally unconcerned smile.

I groaned and stalked out of the room and onto the

street, where I asked B.B. to get me my bike, throwing in a 'please' and everything. Hot tears stung at my eyes as I raced off. I wasn't sure whether they were tears of humiliation or regret. Ten thousand dollars. I'd just turned down ten thousand dollars.

But what was I supposed to do? Those girls needed someone to tell them that they couldn't just throw money around and buy people. They couldn't have anything they wanted – especially not me. I was never going to take anything from Carina or Ingrid as long as I lived.

It wasn't until I was halfway to the Take Five Lighting offices that I realised I was still wearing a cashmere sweater and that I had a $500 price tag plastered to my sweaty back.

You're going to get this job and bring home a pay cheque and everything will be fine, I told myself as I sat in the outer office at Take Five. *You don't need their stupid money.*

Of course, what I'd seen of Take Five so far didn't exactly have me psyched to work there. The receptionist's desk was piled with papers and surrounded by cardboard boxes overflowing with files. There were paths cut between towers of boxes that were barely big enough to slip through sideways. I was sitting on an old orange couch next to a lamp, a dead potted plant, and what looked like some kind of rotting fruit in a bowl. The smell was not appealing.

The door to the nearly blocked-in office across from me opened and a frazzled-looking man with a comb-over stuck his head out.

'Julia Johnson!' he shouted.

I jumped up and walked into his office, where he promptly slammed the door.

'Have a seat,' he said, gesturing at me with a file. I looked around, but there didn't appear to be any chairs in the office – just more boxes. I finally opted to lean back against a filing cabinet and hope he didn't notice that I wasn't sitting. I wanted every last thing to go right. I *needed* every last thing to go right.

'Okay,' the man said, sitting behind his desk. 'We need help moving out of this office and into a bigger one on the other side of town. Somebody's gonna have to reorganise all the files. It's gonna be hard work.'

'I'm not afraid of hard work,' I said, plastering a smile on my face.

'Good. I like that in a girl,' the man said, looking me up and down in a way that made my skin crawl. Suddenly I realised that he hadn't even told me his name and no one knew where I was. Smooth move for the girl with the 4.0 GPA.

'Now, for the first few weeks the hours are going to be long,' the man told me, shuffling through some papers. 'That gonna be a problem?'

I swallowed hard and tried to keep the smile on my face. 'How long?' I asked.

'Oh, you'll be outta here by ten, ten-thirty on weekdays,' he said casually.

'Ten . . . thirty?' Was he serious? Couldn't he tell I was in high school? When was I supposed to study? Not only that, but I couldn't ride my bike through downtown L.A. at ten-thirty at night. My mom would freak.

'Um . . . any way that can be . . . negotiated?' I asked, my heart pounding.

The man slapped his papers down and fixed his beady little eyes on me. 'You want this job or not?' he asked.

At that moment, I was thinking not.

By the time I got home, I was exhausted. I chained my bike to the rail at the bottom of the stairwell and trudged up the stairs, craving my favourite pyjamas. All I wanted to do was go to bed and forget about this crappy day. I pushed the door open and headed straight for my room but paused in the hallway when I heard a noise coming from the kitchen. My heart dropped when I realised what it was.

My mom was crying. I hesitated for a split second, my stomach tightening into a sickening knot. My mother didn't get upset very easily, but when she did, I always felt like a helpless two-year-old. I held my breath and walked into the kitchen.

She was sitting at the table in her uniform, chewing on the side of her thumbnail, her big wet eyes staring straight ahead. She had a crumpled-up tissue in one hand and her face was streaked with tears. Desperate circled around her legs, clawing at her stockings, meowing in distress, as though realising that the crying meant no one was going to think to feed her anytime soon.

'Mom?' I said, my voice small. 'Are you okay?'

She looked over at me, surprised, then sniffled and wiped her hands across her face.

'Hey, sweetie,' she said, trying to smile. 'How was your day?'

'Mom, who cares?' I asked, sitting down across from her at the table. 'What's going on?'

She sighed and lifted her arms, revealing a crisp-looking white envelope. She pressed her fingertips into it and slid it across the wooden tabletop towards me. I had a feeling I already knew what it was.

'You might as well read it,' my mother said. She looked down. 'I'm really sorry, hon.'

My stomach clenching, I opened the envelope and drew out a letter. I made myself read the words.

Yup, an eviction notice. If we didn't turn in all our back rent *and* next month's within two weeks, we'd have to move *out* in two weeks.

'Mom.' I got up and crouched down next to her chair. 'I'm so sorry.'

She clasped my hand in both of hers. When she looked at me, her eyes were red and puffy. 'What kind of person would kick us out of our home with no warning at all? It just isn't right.'

I felt a wave of guilt crash over me. I had hidden all those letters from my mother to try to keep her from worrying, but all I'd done was make our situation worse. This was my fault.

Desperate meowed again, and I felt a fang dig gently into my ankle. Maybe under her ratty fur she realised she was about to go back to the very streets she thought she'd left behind. Maybe she was wondering why she'd let such losers save her in the first place.

'I even bought some lottery tickets tonight,' my mom said, pulling a few crumpled slips out of her apron pocket. She let out a forced laugh. 'Shockingly enough, we didn't win.'

I smiled and took the tickets from her, balling them up in my hand.

'Oh, honey, what are we going to do?' my mother asked. 'I know I'm supposed to be the mother and tell you—'

'We'll think of something,' I said quickly. 'It'll be okay, Mom. I swear.'

My mother smiled at me, then reached out to grab me up in a quick hug. 'Do I ever tell you what a cool kid you are?' she asked me.

'Like every day,' I replied, letting out a half laugh, half sob.

My mother pulled back and I was about to get up to go to my room for a nice, long think when her brow wrinkled.

'Julia, where did you get that sweater?' she asked.

My stomach sank. 'Uh . . . this?' I asked, standing up. 'I borrowed it from a friend.'

'It's beautiful,' my mother said, reaching up to stroke my arm. She smiled wistfully up at me. 'I'm so glad you have the opportunity to go to that school and meet all those different kinds of people. You have such generous friends.'

Little did she know how generous this particular *friend* was trying to be. A tingly mixture of determination, excitement, and resolve rushed over my skin as I turned to pick up my backpack. I pulled the little white card out of the side pocket and stared down at the phone number written across the back.

I swallowed hard, knowing what I had to do. I was holding winning lottery numbers right in my hand. All I had to do was cash in.

Chapter 8

I opened the door the following evening to find Carina standing there with her hair all pushed up under a Dodgers cap and her face hidden by a pair of oversized sunglasses. She was wearing Diesel jeans, a thin white T-shirt, and Birkenstocks and had a stuffed messenger bag slung over her shoulder.

'Princess,' I said flatly.

'Pauper,' she replied.

I pressed my lips together and opened the door a little wider. She stepped into the living room and stopped short, her mouth dropping open ever so slightly. I felt my face flush, knowing she was shocked by her very unpalacelike surroundings and waiting for her to say something obnoxious. But instead she recovered herself and pulled off the baseball cap and glasses.

'It's . . . nice,' she said.

'Where's Ingrid?' I asked, starting to close the door.

At that moment I heard footsteps barrelling up the stairs and the door was suddenly pushed open – hard. It hit my arm and I tripped back a few steps.

'Oh! Sorry!' Ingrid gasped breathlessly. She clung to both straps of a vinyl backpack. 'Some guy downstairs just tried to sell me a kitten that I think was actually a rat.' She looked both disgusted and also kind of thrilled as she made this announcement.

'That was just Sweaty Luke,' I said, closing the door behind her. 'You didn't touch him, did you?'

'God, no,' Ingrid said, pulling off her linen jacket. 'Why?'

'Don't ask,' I said. 'So, how did you guys get away from the . . . Fröken?'

Ingrid and Carina walked around the coffee table, which was overflowing with old magazines, and perched on the edge of the couch. Carina adjusted her position a few times, looking down at the itchy fabric that covered the cushion as if it was going to bite her. Finally she found a spot without a spring under it.

'They're giving us three hours off in the evenings so B.B. can take us to all the cultural places,' Ingrid replied. 'La Brea Tar Pits, the Los Angeles Symphony, the Getty Museum . . .'

'How'd you get him to bring you here instead?' I asked.

'We don't call him Buyable Bill for nothing, remember?' Ingrid said.

'Right,' I replied, trying not to think of how very buyable I'd turned out to be.

From the corner of my eye I saw Desperate trot out from the kitchen. Suddenly she jumped up on the back of the sofa and Carina flew out of her seat, letting out a scream.

'What *is* that thing?' she wailed, her hand to her chest.

I laughed, walked over, and picked up Desperate in my arms. 'It's my cat,' I replied, stroking her mangy fur lovingly. Definitely a bad fur day. I looked at Carina's distressed expression and smirked. 'Maybe we should go into my room. It's the second door down the hall.'

Carina swallowed hard, then followed Ingrid towards my bedroom, which, I'll admit, I'd tidied up for the evening's activities. The moment they were out of hearing range, I lifted Desperate up in front of me and looked her in the eye.

'Good cat.'

She purred in response.

'Let's get started,' Ingrid said, dumping out her backpack onto my bed. Half a dozen hardcover books spilled out. The smell of the musty pages filled my nostrils and the bookworm in me got a little thrill. I'm such a nerd.

'You'll need to study these,' Carina said, making a neat little pile out of the books. 'There will be a lot of dignitaries at the ball and you'll be expected to know everything there is to know about Vineland.'

'What do they do, quiz you?' I asked, sitting down on my bed and picking up one of the heavier books.

'No, but you'd be surprised how often the average yearly rainfall comes up in conversation,' Carina said, rolling her eyes. 'I'm constantly surrounded by deathly boring people.'

I opened the book to the glossy section of pictures near the back, depicting kings, queens, princes, and princesses of Vineland throughout the ages. None of them looked all that boring to me.

'Is this your mother?' Carina asked, picking up a

framed photo from my dresser. It had been taken when I was ten and my mother had got a couple of discount tickets to Disneyland. We'd waited almost an hour to pose with Mickey, but it was one of my favourite memories.

'Yep,' I said. 'Not the one with the big ears.'

Carina smiled slightly. 'She's pretty.'

'I know,' I said.

'Where is she tonight?' Carina asked.

'Working,' I told her. 'She's working every night this week and all day Saturday.' Luckily, that meant it was going to be easy for me to play princess that weekend. Unluckily, it meant I was barely going to see my mother for the next few days. I hated that.

'Sounds like my father,' Carina said, a distinct bitterness in her voice.

Yeah, but your dad works in a tux and signs treaties with kings. My mom works in polyester and gets her butt pinched by drunks all night, I thought with an equal amount of bitterness.

'I've always wanted to go to an amusement park,' Carina said wistfully, putting the picture down and moving on to the photo album next to it. Meanwhile, Ingrid was absently leafing through a pile of papers on my desk – scholarship forms, job listings, SAT locations. Plus the many, many money-grubbing notes from the landlord that I'd hidden from my mom. She was reading them as if it didn't even occur to her that they were my private things.

'You've never been to an amusement park?' I asked, jumping up and snatching the papers from Ingrid's hands. She looked surprised but unperturbed. I crossed over to Carina, opened my junk drawer, and started to shove the papers in, but Carina's eyes widened slightly and she grabbed something from the drawer.

'*You* have a passport?' she asked, opening the little blue booklet and checking out the truly heinous picture. I grabbed that back from her as well. 'There aren't any stamps in it,' she pointed out.

'Yeah, well, I've never been anywhere,' I replied, shoving everything back in the drawer and slamming it shut.

'So then why do you have a passport?' Ingrid asked, leaning in towards my full-length mirror to check out the pictures of my friends that were shoved in under the fake gold rim.

I was starting to get a little fed up with this visit. 'If you must know, I got it a couple of years ago. My mom and I had a fight and I told her I was going to run away to Mexico. She didn't believe me, so I used all my savings to get a passport to prove I was serious.' I took a deep breath and flopped down on my bed. 'Little did I know, you don't need a passport to go to Mexico, and I didn't have the money to get there anyway. By the time it came in the mail, we'd long since made up.'

Carina smirked and looked at Ingrid. 'Sounds like something I would do.'

'She's had many botched escapes,' Ingrid clarified, turning away from the mirror. She bent over Carina's bag and opened the flap, revealing a buffet of styling products. She started to sort through them, laying lipsticks, powders, tiny little pots of something or other, and a few random tools on my desk.

'Why would you try to escape?' I asked, looking down at

the book on my bed. It was open to a two-page aerial view of the castle. The place looked like something out of a dream.

Carina gazed down at it and breathed out slowly. 'You would, too, if your parents wouldn't take you to an amusement park.' She reached out and closed the book. 'Or anywhere else you ever wanted to go.'

I looked up at Carina, and for that split second I saw something reflected in her eyes – a sort of sorrow. And it wasn't a 'poor-me' sorrow. It was an 'I'm-trapped' sorrow. I knew the feeling well. Whenever I overheard the girls in my class planning group ski trips to Aspen or weekends at the spa. Whenever they turned to me with those looks in their eyes like they felt so sorry for me that their parents were able to give them everything and my mom wasn't.

'Okay, we're ready!' Ingrid said, clapping and striking a pose disturbingly similar to an evil scientist's. 'I'll be in charge of the tweezing, waxing, exfoliating, toning, and moisturising while Carina helps you study.'

Ingrid got out a huge clip and started pinning my hair back from my face.

'Um,' I said.

'Trust me,' she said.

I bit my lower lip. 'Okay,' I said.

Ingrid grinned, her eyes practically glowing with mischief. 'Let's get to work.'

Chapter 9

From: princessgirl@vineland.org
To: rockmyworld@aol.com

I can't believe it's really happening! Only five more days until we actually meet! I'm counting the hours. Meanwhile, I'm really loving L.A. It has all the sand I imagined and twice the number of palm trees. It's like all my dreams are really coming true.

From: rockmyworld@aol.com
To: princessgirl@vineland.org

can't wait to meet you either . . . have to go to rehersil now . . . we have a few new songs i know you'll luv . . . maybe i'll dedicate one to ya!!!!! later babe!!!!!

The phone in my hotel room rang, jarring me out of a vivid daydream of Ribbit bringing me up onto the stage during the concert, pulling me to his sweaty chest, and telling everyone, 'This is the girl who inspired my new song. And I love her.' In the dream Markus sat in the front row looking up at us all devastated, realising what he could have had if he wasn't such a boring little snob. I grabbed the receiver and barked a 'hello'.

'Is that any way for a princess to answer the telephone?' my mother said. But she sounded teasing, not annoyed.

For a split second I almost wished she were there with me. I knew how much she would enjoy eating all the good food and walking around in the sun, being surrounded by people who looked like they'd fallen straight out of the movies we loved watching together. But of course if she were there, she wouldn't be so fond of some of my other activities – like, oh, say, prepping Julia so that she could take my place at some important gatherings while I ran off to a concert and met up with a rock star who I'd met on the Internet. I quickly came back down to earth.

'Hello, Mother,' I said, leaning back in my chair.

'How is everything going on your trip, Carina?' my mother asked. 'It's been so long since I've heard from you.'

'We're having a great time,' I answered, ready to share the things I could. 'Today we toured Universal Studios and the head of the studio gave us tickets to a premiere tomorrow night at Mann's Chinese Theatre – you know, the one where they *always* hold premieres? I think Ben Affleck is going to be there! Oh, and it's so beautiful, the palm trees and the ocean and the mountains! And Mom, today I had the best smoothie I have ever tasted in my life. I got the recipe so we could give it to the new cook. You're gonna love it.'

I paused for breath, figuring my mother would comment on *something* I had just said. After all, she was the one who had predicted that Ben Affleck would be a huge star after we'd rented *Good Will Hunting*, although she had *not* approved of the language in that film. But there was total silence.

'What's the matter?' I asked.

'Have you gone to the naked beach?' my mother asked, sounding far more serious than she had before.

'There is no naked beach, Mother!' I grabbed a pencil and made a note on the hotel stationery: *Check on the naked beach!*

'Just remember where you came from,' she said. 'Remember who you are.'

My insides went all hot and queasy when she said that to me. Did she think I was still five years old?

'It's kind of hard to forget,' I said.

'Carina.' She sounded very tired. 'I don't understand you. Don't you realise how lucky you are? How many people would give their lives to be in your shoes? Don't you realise all the good you can do with your life?'

Guilt. Guiltguiltguilt. Guilt.

'Mom, I'm kind of tired,' I said, pulling my knees up under my chin and resting my face on the silky fabric of my pyjamas. I wanted to get off the phone and get back to my Ribbit daydream

There was a long pause.

'Are you going to even ask about her?' my mother said finally.

My stomach turned. 'How is Grandmamma?' I asked.

'She's taken a turn for the worse,' my mother replied.

'I'm going to have to go to the hospital and stay with her.'

'Oh.' I didn't know what else to say.

'You could call her, at least,' my mother said.

More guilt.

'I will,' I said impatiently. She was making my stomach hurt.

'When?'

Guiltguiltguilt. I was too young and too . . . *far away* to deal with this.

'Soon,' I lied.

After a few more warnings about my behaviour, my mother and I hung up. I stood up and walked over to the window, drawing the shade aside. The view of the beach was breathtaking. The palm trees swayed in the breeze as the waves crashed and rolled and hissed. The moon hung low in the sky, casting a glittering shadow on the ripples far out against the horizon.

Somewhere out there Ribbit was rehearsing his new songs and thinking of me. A tingle of excitement raced down my spine, and I pulled the pink silk of my robe closer to me. I wished I could just freeze time right then and there. Then I could keep feeling this euphoric antici-pation of meeting Ribbit and how perfect it would be. Then I could stay in California for ever and live just like a normal girl. (If I could get rid of Killjoy, of course.)

If I could freeze time, my grandmother would never die and my mother wouldn't have to be sad all the time. There would be no more guilt to throw around.

The door to the suite opened and Ingrid walked in and flopped down onto my bed. 'How's Frog Man?' she asked.

I smiled. Just hearing his name, or Ingrid's approxima-
tion of it, was enough to snap me out of my deep thoughts.
I was not going to dwell on my parental issues right now.

'Ingrid,' I said. 'I think I'm in love.'

The moment I said it, a warm, fuzzy feeling over came
me and I knew it was true. I grinned and hopped onto the
bed next to her.

'I'm in love with a guy I've never even met!' I said,
giggling.

'Oh my God, I've never seen you like this,' Ingrid said.
She sat up and levelled me with a pretend-serious stare.
'What would Markus think?'

'Who cares about Markus,' I said, grinning. 'Markus
the Great has nothing on Ribbit the Greater.' I pulled one
of the feather pillows onto my lap and sighed. 'How cool
would it be if some reporter took a picture of me and
Ribbit together? Can you just imagine Markus's face?
You know it would make the cover of *Inside*.'

'Forget Markus, your parents would kill you,' Ingrid said.
'And they'd probably bring back public hangings for Ribbit.'

'I know,' I said. 'I just . . . sometimes I just wish I
could, I don't know, just say . . . forget about them!' At
that moment, I felt like I could do something rebellious
and crazy, just to show my parents I was capable of being
my own person. But in the back of my mind, I knew it
would never happen. I was too afraid of disappointing
them. And I hated it.

'I wish you could go with me to the concert,' I told
Ingrid. 'It would be so much more fun.'

'Trust me, I'd rather go with you than baby-sit Julia all

night,' Ingrid said, rolling over onto her stomach and propping her chin up on a pillow. 'But someone has to be there to make sure the new princess uses the right fork.'

'I really appreciate this, Ingrid,' I told her. 'You have no idea how much.'

'Don't worry about it,' she said, looking up at me. 'I'll make the sacrifice. It's worth it to get you away from Markus.'

I couldn't argue with that. Poor Julia was going to be stuck doing the long-arm waltz with Markus all night while I got up close and personal with Ribbit.

'Carina, I think Julia and her mom are going to lose their home,' Ingrid said suddenly.

'What?' I asked, my forehead wrinkling. 'Why?'

'Yesterday in her room I saw these notes that said the rent was past due. There was something about taking . . . *serious measures*,' Ingrid said.

'What does that mean?' I asked.

'I don't know, but it does not sound good,' Ingrid replied. 'They must be, like, *really* poor. I feel like we should do something.'

I reached forward and felt Ingrid's forehead. 'Are you feeling okay?' I asked. 'You've never felt like you should *do* something before in your entire life.'

Ingrid laughed it off and shook her head. 'You're right. I don't know what's wrong with me. It's like being in L.A. has made me all philanthropic or whatever.'

I sighed. Julia's apartment was small and it had an odd, mouldy sort of smell, like the canals in Venice – Italy, not L.A. But it was clean, and she went to a good school. She couldn't be *that* poor.

'Well, at least the money we're giving her will help,' I said, picking at the lace on the pillowcase. I couldn't even imagine what it would feel like to *need* ten thousand dollars. It had cost more than twice that to renovate my bathroom last year. 'Do you think she's going to do a good job being me?' I asked.

'Julia? Too early to tell.'

'Well, she *is* a fast study,' I said, recalling how quickly Julia had picked up all the little facts about my family and my country. 'I can just imagine how psyched Heinrich the Lisper would be to get her as a student. He might even be spurred into completing a whole thought.'

Ingrid laughed.

I felt a twinge of something unpleasant in my stomach at the memory of Julia rattling off Vineland trivia as if she'd lived there her entire life, but I squelched it. What was wrong with me? I should have been happy that we'd found such a capable girl for the job. So long as we tamed that rat's nest she called hair, everything would be perfect.

'What's on the agenda for tomorrow night?' I asked.

'Table manners. Waltzing. Other forms of etiquette,' Ingrid said, counting the items off on her fingers.

'Sounds like fun,' I said, rolling my eyes. 'I'll be impressed if we can even get her to sit up straight.'

Just then Fröken Killjoy came busting through the door without knocking, sniffing the air as though trying to detect a wisp of smoke. Her face was covered in a blue exfoliating night mask and her hair was up in curlers.

'Lights out, girls,' she said.

'Fröken Killroy!' Ingrid said, standing up right next to

the woman and inspecting her face. 'What's with the products? Are you . . . primping for someone?'

I stifled a smile and tried to look innocently interested in a reply. Ingrid and I had seen Killjoy talking with the American ambassador to Vineland earlier that afternoon and had almost convulsed with laughter. The ambassador was an older, distinguished man with salt-and-pepper hair and twinkling eyes – not bad for a near geriatric. Fröken had spent the entire conversation tossing her hair and giggling like . . . well . . . like us.

'Nonsense, girls,' Fröken Killroy said, stuffing her hands under her arms. 'I just want to look my best. We are here representing our country.'

'Of course,' I said. 'And I'm sure Ambassador Rivers appreciates the effort.'

'Well . . . uh . . . I . . . excuse me, girls,' Killjoy said. Then she pulled the collar of her robe up around her chin and rushed from the room.

Ingrid and I cracked up laughing the moment the door was closed.

'I think Fröken Killroy is smitten,' Ingrid said. 'I *told* you she just needed a guy to smooch.'

'Ugh! Oh! Oh nooo! Now I have a mental picture of Killroy kissing *Rivers*!' I picked up a pillow and threw it at Ingrid's head.

'Oh no, you did not!' Ingrid cried, grabbing another pillow.

She whacked me across the face with it, and soon we were engaged in a laughing, shrieking, full-out war. By the time we were done, panting and dishevelled, I was exhausted. Ingrid decided to stay over in my room and we crawled under the covers, ready for a nice, long, sleep.

As I drifted off to sleep, I went back to my Ribbit fantasies, hoping that if I thought about him enough, I'd dream about him as well. And I did. In the dream I was at his concert with curlers in my hair and holding Julia's big smelly hat, but none of it mattered because Ribbit was singing up on-stage. A love song.

And there was no one in the audience but me.

Chapter 10

Thursday afternoon I sat in the library at school, chewing on my fingernails and studying yet another book about Vineland. I'd never been much of a nail biter and it was really kind of gross, but Carina's nails were bitten down to her fingertips, so now mine had to be, too. Some princess. You'd think she'd have had an official manicurist following her around, smacking her hand every time it went near her mouth. But Ingrid assured me that everyone in Vineland expected Carina not to have nails. Apparently it was one of her most beloved quirks. There was a top ten list of them in *Vineland Today* last year. Also on the list was the way she refused to eat carrots or any food that had touched a carrot.

Freaky.

At least the book I had brought to school was interesting enough to distract me from the ickiness of what I was doing to my hands. It described every last room of the Vineland palace in detail and was crammed with about a million pictures.

I turned the page and my breath caught in my throat.

There, covering two whole pages, was a huge, glossy picture of the most beautiful library I had ever seen. The walls were as high as a cathedral and they were lined with books all the way up to the ceiling. There were winding staircases leading up to walkways that ran along the shelves, where a few men in tuxedos and sashes gazed up at the millions of tomes. The wooden railings and bookshelves gleamed and the tile floor shone under the light of a huge chandelier.

I could only imagine how incredible the books must be there and how perfect and hushed and still a library like that would be.

I turned the page again and was faced with a photo of Carina waltzing with a guy about our age in the centre of a gilded ballroom. Hundreds of people looked on from the edges of the dance floor. Carina wore a flowing gown of soft pinks and corals and her hair was gathered up behind a sparkling diamond tiara. She looked . . . well, like a princess. But as she gazed at the guy who was holding her, she also looked . . . bored.

I glanced at the guy and immediately I could tell why. He was tall and had dark hair and that kind of chiselled face you expect a prince to have. His mouth was twisted into a cocky smirk, and his head was held at this slight angle that just screamed, 'My goodness, I'm really quite good looking, aren't I? Oh yes, I just love myself.'

Men. He probably thought he was just so special because he was dancing with a princess. I was about to slap the book shut on his smirky little face when the caption caught my eye.

Princess Carina dances with the son of the duke of Vasta, Markus Ingvaldsson, her boyfriend.

Her . . . her . . . her . . .

'What?' I shouted, throwing the book down.

Carina had a boyfriend? She hadn't told me that! Was this Markus jerk going to be at the ball? Was he going to expect me to dance with him in front of everyone like that? Was he going to expect me to . . . *kiss* him?

Suddenly I felt an intense need for some fresh air. I packed up my stuff and headed for my bike.

Okay, stay calm, I told myself as I rode towards home. Maybe Carina hadn't mentioned Markus for a reason. Maybe he wasn't even going to *be* at the ball. Or maybe he wasn't really her boyfriend – people always exaggerated that stuff when it came to celebrities, right? What was it my mother always said? 'Don't stress about something until you know there's something to stress about.'

Of course, that had backfired on her big time when I'd hidden all those warning notices from her. I felt the guilt start to seep over me again but tried to soothe it with the thought that soon I was going to have ten thousand dollars. And my mother would have nothing to worry about.

I should probably start thinking about how I'm going to explain that, I realised.

I turned down Abbot Kinney, as I often did on my way home, just to check the window at Sasha's and see if my mother's hats were displayed. The sun beat down and I wondered if I should start carrying sunscreen around with me. I didn't think Carina would appreciate it if I showed up for the ball with a sunburn.

I jumped the kerb and rode on the sidewalk until I got to Sasha's. A bunch of my mother's creations were displayed in the window, and I smiled when I saw a salesgirl lift one of them up to show a customer. The hats were all so beautiful and all priced too low. Feathered hats, felt hats, hats made of mesh. White hats, purple hats, hats in all the colours of the rainbow.

When I got my ten thousand dollars, I was going to buy every last one of my mother's hats and pay triple for them. It was so wrong that my mother wasn't a famous designer. Just because some jerk swept her off her feet and made her forget what she really wanted to do with her life and then left her broke and broken-hearted. Some jerk called my father.

Moral of the story? Never let a guy interfere with your dreams.

I rode home at double speed and took the steps two at a time, resolving to call Carina and find out exactly what the deal was with this Markus guy. I wasn't sure what I was going to say, exactly, if she did tell me I had to kiss him and whisper sweet nothings to him or call him 'Pookie' or 'Darling Pie' or whatever else people with boyfriends did. But the very thought of kissing someone I didn't know – of kissing some egotistical *snob* I didn't know – made me wonder if ten thousand dollars was enough money.

Guys. Were they ever *not* causing trouble?

I opened the door to our apartment and stepped on yet another envelope. My heart dropped down to my toes. What was this? A we-just-wanted-to-rub-your-eviction-in-your-face notice?

I picked the envelope up with shaking hands, and when I opened it, I almost dropped it on the floor. I couldn't even believe my own eyes. Inside was a stack of money! I reached in and pulled out the bills – so crisp and new they were sticking to each other. A little piece of paper fell out and fluttered to the floor. I grabbed it up and read it quickly.

J. –

   My dad always says that if you pay half up front, the job will be done to your satisfaction. Don't spend it all in one place.

                          – *I. (& C.)*

Half? Up front? Was I really holding five thousand dollars in my hand right now?

There was a knock at the door and I shoved the money into the back pocket of my jeans. I opened the door to find Dominic, the super, sucking his teeth on my doorstep.

'Just wanted to make sure you're packin' up,' he said, clicking his tongue. 'Mr Frontz, you know, the new *landlord*, wanted me to check.'

'Do you have any idea what a jerk you are?' I blurted before I could stop myself.

He blinked, taken aback for a split second, then drew himself up to his full, semi-intimidating height. 'Call me when they start carting out your stuff. I wanna watch,' he said.

I narrowed my eyes at him. 'Can you just wait there for one second?' I asked. Then I turned and ducked into the kitchen.

My hands shaking, I pulled the money out of my back

pocket and quickly counted out a bunch of hundreds. I shoved the rest back where it came from and paused. Should I do this? But then, why not? It was my money, right? And this was why I had earned it. Or was *going* to earn it.

Before I could think it through a couple hundred times, I came back to the door and held up the money. Dominic's eyes widened and he froze, so I grabbed his grimy hand, pulled it towards me, and slapped the money into his palm.

'There's enough there for August, September, *and* October,' I told him. 'You can bring me a receipt in the morning.'

He opened his mouth, but no sound came out. I slammed the door right in his face.

The second I was alone, I started to laugh. Had I really just done that? Huh. Maybe there was a little Carina in me after all.

Chapter 11

'Repeat after me,' Carina ordered. 'I am pleased to meet you and I speak for all of Vineland when I say that we appreciate your country's support.'

'I am pleased to meet you,' I repeated, trying to match her Frenchish/Swedishish accent. 'And I speak—'

'No, no, no,' Ingrid interrupted. 'Be a little more affected. Think Madonna.'

'I am pleased to—'

'No!' Carina snapped. 'I don't sound like that! And Julia, you have to sit up straight.'

I sighed and straightened my back, trying not to let my blood get over the boiling point. *Just think about the look on Dominic's face when you handed him that money,* I told myself. *You would never have been able to do that without these people.*

'Maybe we should take a break,' Ingrid said, picking up the phone by the bed. 'Room service, anyone?'

I shook my head. 'Listen, you guys, I just wanted to thank you for leaving me that money,' I said, furrowing my brow when I saw Ingrid gesturing wildly with the phone behind Carina's back. 'It was really—'

'What money?' Carina asked.

She turned around to look at Ingrid, who immediately slammed down the phone, her cheeks flushed.

'What money?' Carina repeated.

'I kind of . . . went over there the other day when you were doing that press conference and left Julia half the money,' Ingrid said in a rush.

'You did *what*?'

'You didn't know?' I asked.

'What's the big deal?' Ingrid said, lifting her shoulders. 'It was just . . . good business. My father always says—'

'The big deal is you told me you were going to Fred Segal,' Carina said. 'The big deal is you lied to me. Nobody lies to me.'

'Carina, people lie to you all the time,' Ingrid said flatly.

'Um . . . maybe I should—'

'How much did you give her?' Carina demanded, ignoring me. 'She hasn't even *done* anything yet.'

Suddenly I felt like I had been slapped in the face. 'Hold on a sec, I haven't *done* anything? I've been hanging out with you guys every single day after school when I *should* be studying for my classes, but instead I've been learning all about your stupid little country. I've been plucked, I've been tweezed, I've been biting off my nails!' I flung up my hand to show them the raw skin and the jagged cuticles. 'How can you say I haven't done anything?'

Carina took a deep breath and sat down on the edge of her bed. 'Repeat after me,' she said, clearly struggling to control her temper. 'I am pleased to meet you and I speak for all of Vineland when I say—'

'I am pleased to meet you and I speak for all of Los Angeles when I say you are a total bitch,' I snapped, crossing my arms over my chest.

Ingrid let out a loud guffaw, then slapped her hand over her mouth.

There were a few long moments of silence and then, to my total shock, Carina started laughing. Seconds later Ingrid joined her, and before long, I felt a laugh welling up inside my throat as well. It was a complete tension reliever. Carina bent over at the waist, holding her stomach.

'I . . . I can't believe you just said that,' she said, catching her breath. She wiped a tear away from her eye with her fingertip and looked at Ingrid. 'You know, I think she might actually do okay.'

A few hours later we were kicking back poolside at the hotel, with Carina's security people stationed along the perimeter of the patio. The pool closed at eight but apparently stayed open for the princess after that. We were sipping virgin piña coladas and enjoying the warm night air. The last thing I wanted to do was get on my bike and ride home, but I was going to have to leave pretty soon if I didn't want to be exhausted at school the next day.

I placed my glass down on the table next to me and sat up. There was something I needed to know before I spent another entire night stressing.

'Carina? Who's Markus?' I asked. I'd wanted to bring him up earlier, but with all the fighting and then the non-stop etiquette lessons, there had never been a good time.

Carina took a deep breath. 'Markus is a guy my parents

want me to marry,' she said, looking out at the glimmering water of the pool.

'What's he like?' I asked.

'Well, he's . . . nice,' Carina said with a shrug. 'Handsome, polite . . . all the mothers love him.'

'And he's a polo *god*,' Ingrid put in sarcastically. She and Carina shared a personal joke-type laugh.

'He sounds great,' I said, raising my eyebrows. Oh God. I was going to have to kiss this guy, wasn't I?

'If you like bland cookie-cutter guys who don't know how to carry on a decent conversation and will never do a single thing that wasn't mapped out for them at birth, then yes – he's great,' Carina said.

I hadn't heard so many words come out of her mouth at one time. She basically seemed so . . . reserved. But then, maybe she was just better at thinking before she spoke than I was.

'So are you going to?' I asked. 'Marry him, I mean.'

'Not if I can help it,' she answered.

She sounded determined and resigned at the same time – as if she knew she didn't want the guy but was sure she was going to end up with him anyway.

'So is he going to be at the ball?' I asked.

'So they tell me,' Carina replied.

'Don't worry about it,' Ingrid said. 'Just avoid him as much as possible. That's what Carina always does.'

'Really?' I asked.

'I'll put it this way,' Carina said, sitting up and gracefully swinging her legs to the side of the chair so she could face me. She leaned her elbows on her knees and looked me right in the eye. 'The more you can do to make Markus less interested in me, the better off we'll *all* be.'

'I'll second that,' Ingrid said smiling to herself behind Carina's back.

'So I don't have to dance with him or kiss him or flirt with him or anything?' I asked, just to be sure.

'Julia, you don't even have to talk to him,' Carina said. 'It's not like my parents are going to be around to make you.'

I smiled. This ball thing was sounding better already.

It is a princess's job to look happy even if she's not.

A princess never has lipstick on her teeth. It should never leave the lip line, and if it does, it will be punished.

A princess never uses swear-words, at least not in public.

A princess never shows more skin than absolutely necessary, at least not in public.

A princess never pulls out her own chair.

A princess always waves with her right hand, held up parallel to the shoulder, moving the hand back and forth at a thirty-eight-degree angle.

A princess always looks surprised when someone asks for her autograph.

A princess always cuts her food into very small pieces. This prevents choking and therefore ending up on the cover of Inside *with your gagging face on.*

A princess glides. She never lumbers.

A princess must look fascinated at all times, even when the conversation is about polo or oil prices.

A princess's tiara is her umbrella.

Chapter 12

That night I gave up on trying to sleep and went to the kitchen to get myself some milk. Not only did I have a million Vineland facts running through my head, but I kept daydreaming about all the different ways I could blow off Carina's Prince Not So Charming. Should I dance with every other guy in the room right in front of him? (Nah. That would require dancing.) Should I tell him off in some grand public spectacle? (Nah. I had a feeling that would put me on the cover of *Inside* faster than choking would.)

Maybe I would just be aloof and ignore him right to his handsome, smug, bland little face. Yeah. That was the ticket.

As I sat down with my glass of milk at the kitchen table, I heard the lock to the front door slide free and my mother come in. She trudged into the kitchen and didn't even register surprise to find me there.

'Hey, hon,' she said wearily.

The front of her waitress outfit was covered with buffalo wing sauce, and she looked like she had run thirty miles. Her hair was plastered to her forehead in various places and her make-up was all but gone.

'Bad night,' she said. 'Looks like the Dodgers have decided not to make the play-offs.'

She dumped her tips out on the table and I felt a lump in my throat. My mother was working her tail off to try to save our apartment, oblivious to the fact that it was already saved. I had a receipt under my pillow proving that I had paid the rent through to October, along with the rest of the cash Ingrid had left me. Crisp, clean hundred-dollar bills very unlike the crumpled ones and fives lying in front of me on the table.

'How was your day?' my mother asked, sweeping her palm over the top of my head as she walked to the sink. She placed a glass under the tap and turned on the water.

I had to tell her. I had to tell her about the money so that she could stop killing herself like this. But what was I going to say? I hadn't the smallest hint of an idea how to explain it. And even if I told her the truth, she would never let me go through with it. Running around pretending to be someone else with a bunch of random strangers was not a protective mother's idea of an acceptable night out for her daughter.

'It was fine,' I said, reaching for a few of the bills and flattening them on the table. They smelled like beer. 'We had a pop quiz in French, but I believe I did quite well.'

The water cut off abruptly. 'Why are you talking like that?' she asked.

'Like what?' I replied, my pulse suddenly pounding. The words were still hanging in the air – *'I believe I did quite well'* – tinged with a Vinelandish accent. 'How am I talking, Mom?' I added, struggling to sound like myself.

She came around the table and looked at me, confused. 'I don't know, I swear you had a funny accent for a minute there.'

I didn't answer. I didn't even move.

She smirked and shook her head. 'I must just be really tired,' she said, wiping her forehead. 'I'm gonna go to bed, sweetie.' She leaned over and planted a kiss on top of my head, then clomped off towards her room.

I'm just going to have to wait until it's over, I thought. *It's only two more days. Then I'll have all the money, and I'll tell her what I did, and she'll ground me for life, but at least she won't be able to keep me from finishing what I started.*

I gathered up the rest of my mother's tips and counted them carefully. Eighty-two dollars. If the So-Cal teams kept running themselves into the ground, we were really going to need the rest of the princess money.

And I'd heard the Lakers were going to suck this year, too.

Chapter 13

From: princessgirl@vineland.org
To: rockmyworld@aol.com

Ribbit,

Thanks so much for offering to have one of your roadies pick me up behind the embassy on Saturday. I'm counting the hours!

I went to Tower Records on Sunset today and bought all your CDs so that I would know every single song by heart for the concert. I just have to say, you are a musical genius! And your lyrics are just so . . . inspiring. Especially on your romantic songs, like "Your Love Is a Trojan Horse" and "Bad Love Gone Worse". You must be the most sensitive man in the world. Please forgive me for going on like this; I just feel like something magical is happening, and I can't wait for the concert, when our eyes first meet.

From: rockmyworld@aol.com
To: princessgirl@vineland.org

im drunk.

I leaned back in the rickety chair in Julia's kitchen, staring at Ribbit's response on my laptop. My heart felt like it had been pierced. Here I had gone and poured my guts out to him and he had, well, *not*.

But he's a rock star, I told myself. *Of course he parties while he's on tour.*

People probably thought the same thing about me – that when I came to L.A., I would go to all the hottest clubs and chill in the VIP rooms drinking Cristal. Imagine what the breathless public would think if they knew I was sitting in a hovel with a mangy cat rubbing her matted fur against my ankle. Not only that, but Ben Affleck hadn't even shown up for that movie premiere that afternoon. The biggest star I had seen was the kid from *Malcolm in the Middle*. Totally lame. Although I *had* really liked him in that movie *My Dog Skip*.

'Are you ready yet?' I called out, causing the cat to jump.

'Just give us one more minute!' Ingrid called from the bedroom, where she was putting the finishing touches on her 'greatest masterpiece', Julia. 'Carina, she looks just like you!'

I rolled my eyes even as my face flushed. Ingrid had been showing off all day about the transformation she was going to orchestrate and I had been telling *her* all day that she was utterly loco. As much as I wanted this to work, I knew deep down that no one was ever going to believe that Julia Johnson was me. It was completely impossible.

Only I can be me. Right?

I closed the e-mail window on my computer and

rested my chin in my hand – a posture that Killjoy and my mother would *not* approve of. Who would be at the embassy ball tomorrow night? Most likely a lot of people whom I'd only met once or twice. They would be fooled by Julia's disguise as long as she didn't lose the accent or slurp her soup. Then there was Markus. But he'd probably be too busy kissing old-lady and dignitary butt to notice. I could probably dye my hair purple and he would still say, 'Carina, you look beautiful this evening. Would you do me the honour of a dance?'

Seriously. He *actually* talked like that. So irritating.

At least my parents wouldn't be there. Because my mom would *definitely* know Julia was not me. My dad, of course, was another story. I hadn't seen him in so long that I wasn't sure he'd recognise *me* if I walked right up to him and stepped on his foot.

Huh. So maybe Julia *could* be me. For a night, anyway. I swallowed hard at the thought, trying to calm the nauseous feeling in my stomach. How was it that I could think of only two people – Ingrid and my mother – who would actually be able to tell the difference between the real me and an imposter?

I heard the door to the bedroom open, and Ingrid walked out into the living room, which opened up onto the kitchen. She was practically beaming. For some reason, when I stood up, my knees were shaking. I composed myself and walked around the kitchen table to stand at the edge of the living room.

'Princess Carina,' Ingrid said dramatically, 'I'd like you to meet . . . Princess Carina.'

Then she stepped aside with a flourish of her hand and out walked . . . a mirror. I swear all the oxygen whooshed right out of me the moment I saw Julia. She glided into the centre of the room, walking with perfect grace and dignity in low heels and one of my favourite ball gowns. Her hair, though still brown, was swept up in a bun, with wisps hanging around her face. Her make-up was done just as I preferred mine – light on the eyes with dark, dramatic lips.

My throat went dry and I struggled for something to say. They were both looking at me so expectantly. But this was all just a little too bizarre. I opened my mouth and then—

'I speak for all of Vineland when I say it is truly an honour to be here.'

I hadn't spoken. Julia had. But it might as well have been me. She had my voice down perfectly.

'Freaky, isn't it?' Ingrid said, stepping up next to me to view Julia from my perspective. 'Good thing you got that nose job, C. Otherwise we never could have pulled this off.'

I reached out and grasped the back of the overstuffed chair next to me. Suddenly I started to sweat in a very undignified manner. It was like Julia had been me before I had been me. She was even born with the nose I had *asked* for.

I'm replaceable, I thought suddenly, my stomach turning. *Not only has my life been dictated since the day I was born, but I'm also completely and totally . . . replaceable.*

'Aren't you going to say anything?' Ingrid prodded. Julia bit her lip and looked at me nervously.

'Oh! I know! You need the tiara for full effect,' Ingrid said, reaching for my crown, which sat in the centre of the table in front of the couch.

Just before her fingertips touched the diamonds, I heard myself shout at her. 'No!' I said. She froze and the word just hung in the air. 'Don't touch it!'

'What's the matter?' Ingrid asked, pulling her hand back.

'I . . . I . . .'

I was on the verge of tears.

'This is never going to work,' I blurted, my heart pounding. 'Anyone can tell she's a fraud. *Anyone*. There's no way she can be me.'

I looked at Julia's face again. Bad idea. *She* is *me,* a little voice in my head wailed. *She* is *me!*

Suddenly I couldn't take it any more. I grabbed my tiara and ran out of the apartment, tears streaming down my face. The last time I had cried in public was when my grandfather had died. I barely knew him, but I had been told that it was my duty to shed a few polite tears. Even my emotions weren't truly mine. 'Carina! Wait!' Ingrid called after me as I ran down the stairs.

But I didn't stop. I couldn't. I was angry at Ingrid for taking so much pride in making that girl into a total Carina replacement. I was embarrassed for breaking down in front of them. And I was also totally confused. This was what I wanted, wasn't it? This whole scheme was giving me a chance to meet Ribbit. So why couldn't I stop crying?

'Carina! If you take one more step, I'm taking a picture of you in that little halter top you're wearing and sending it right to your mother's computer!' Ingrid shouted.

I froze in my tracks. 'Why are you even following me?' I asked her, quickly swiping the tears from under my eyes before turning to face her. 'Don't you want to hang out with your little experiment up there?'

'You know, I don't get you at all,' Ingrid said, stepping up in front of me. She had her digital camera in her hand. She must have brought it over to document Julia's historic transformation. 'All I've been trying to do is help you. You really think I *wanted* to spend half my time in L.A. hanging out with your little pauper up there?'

'You're the one who gave her five thousand dollars,' I reminded her. 'I thought you liked the girl.'

Ingrid took a deep breath and looked at the ground. 'Okay, I kinda do, but that's beside the point,' she said. She looked me in the face and her eyes softened. At that moment I knew that she knew what I was thinking. Ingrid might have had a hard exterior and, okay, some hard interior parts as well, but she was still my best friend.

'She's only *playing* you,' she said firmly. 'She's not *replacing* you.'

My heart gave a little thump of doubt. 'I . . . I know that,' I said, not so convincingly.

'No one could ever replace you,' Ingrid said. Then she reached out and hugged me, resting her chin on my shoulder. 'Look, you're going to have the most amazing night of your life with Ribbit and then you're going to come back to the hotel and everything will be normal again. Julia will go back to being Julia and you'll go back to being Carina.'

I pulled away from her and smiled. 'You really think it's going to be the most amazing night of my life?'

'Well, it would be better if *I* was going to be there,' she said. 'But I bet it'll still be all right.'

We both laughed. Ingrid was right. I had to remember why we were doing this. I was going to get to meet Ribbit. I was going to go to a real concert. For one night, I was going to get to be a normal girl. Wasn't that what I'd always wanted?

'Come on,' Ingrid said. 'Let's go back upstairs.'

We started across the sidewalk, but before we made it two steps, Ingrid squeezed my arm, stopping me in my tracks the same way she always did when we were at an event and there was someone undesirable approaching.

'Isn't that Julia's mother?' she said under her breath.

A woman in sneakers and an awful pink-and-white costume approached Julia's building, digging in her purse. She bore a slight resemblance to the pretty woman in the frame in Julia's room.

'I thought she wasn't supposed to be home for hours!' I whispered as the woman pushed through the red door of Julia's building.

'Get in the car!' Ingrid said, opening the door and practically shoving me in. 'B.B.! Honk the horn!' she demanded.

B.B. did as he was told and Julia appeared at the window a few moments later, her expression confused.

'Your mom is coming!' Ingrid half yelled, half whispered.

'What?' Julia shouted.

'Your mom is coming!'

Julia glanced over her shoulder into the apartment, then disappeared.

'If she gets caught in that dress . . . ,' I said, looking up at Julia's window as B.B. pulled out onto the road.

'If she gets caught in that dress,' Ingrid said grimly, 'we're done for.'

Chapter 14

I heard my mother's familiar steps clomping up the stairs and for a second I couldn't move. She was supposed to be working the late shift tonight. What was she doing home? I looked down at my dress, my heart skipping with panic. When her keys hit the doorknob, it was like someone had kicked me in the back. I flew into my room as fast as my tasteful heels would carry me.

'Julia?' my mother called out, sticking her head into the apartment.

'Hi, Mom!' I shouted. I slammed my bedroom door and struggled with the hook at the back of the dress. 'What are you doing home?'

'The place was dead, so they let a few of us off early,' my mom replied, her voice getting closer. The hook finally came free and I unzipped the zipper beneath it. 'Did you eat yet?'

'Uh . . . yeah,' I said, trying not to rip the delicate spaghetti straps as I freed myself from them. The gown fell to the floor and I grabbed an oversized T-shirt off my desk chair, pulling it on quickly just as the door started to open. I yanked out the pins that held my hair back and winced as I tore a few strands right out of my scalp.

Oh God! The gown! I did the only thing I could do and kicked it under the bed.

'What did you make?' my mother asked, leaning against the doorjamb. 'I'm starved.'

'Uh . . . there isn't any left,' I said. Carina and Ingrid had actually brought over Chinese takeout and the containers were piled up in the garbage can under my desk. 'But I could make you some soup or something.' I hustled her out of my room before she could notice the piles of designer make-up and the package of home hair dye we were going to use the following morning. That and the stench of Kung Pao chicken.

'Sounds good,' my mother said as we headed for the kitchen. 'And listen, hon, we need to talk. I'm working all night tomorrow, but I was thinking maybe Sunday we should start packing. Rita said we could move in with her for a few weeks while we find a new place.'

'Great,' I said, wincing. Rita was a friend of my mother's from work. You could smell cigarettes on her from ten feet away, and she also had this annoying thirteen-year-old son named Sheldon who was completely in love with me and showed it by giving me packages of tradable *Star Wars* cards whenever he saw me.

'Look, I know you don't like Rita very much, but I'm out of options here, Julia,' my mother said in her stressed voice. She filled two mugs with water and stuck them in the microwave, then turned to look at me. For the first time I noticed the huge bags under her eyes. 'I don't know what else to do.'

This was ridiculous. I had to tell my mother what was going on. I had to tell her that I'd already solved all our problems.

But she won't let you go through with it, I told myself. *And if you don't go through with it, you'll have to give the money back – money that you don't have any more.*

But I wasn't going to let my mother stay up all night tomorrow worrying about packing and money and the fact that she was going to subject me to the torture of living in a smoke-filled, Sheldon-plagued house. The only problem was, I had no idea what to do.

'I'm surprised there haven't been any new notes from Dominic reminding us of when we have to be out,' my mother said as the microwave beeped. 'Do you think he suddenly grew a conscience?'

A note! I thought suddenly. That was it! It was perfect! Tomorrow before I left, I would leave my mother a note explaining everything, along with the rent receipt and the rest of the money. By the time she got home from work and found it, the ball would be over and it would be too late for her to stop me. I'd still be grounded for ever, but at least she'd get a good night's rest tomorrow night.

'You know what, Mom?' I said as she handed me a mug of steaming water and a tea bag. I smiled as I sat down across from her at the table. 'I have a feeling everything's going to be okay.'

Dear Mom,

You're never going to believe this, but I found a way to raise some money to help us with the rent. I know you're not going to like it, but I swear it's not illegal or dangerous or anything. You know I would never do anything like that. So here's the deal.

This week the princess from Vineland, her name is Carina, came to our school to give a speech. Afterwards I kind of got to meet her and she asked me to help her with something. She wants me to spend the day with her on Saturday and go to this ball that night and then stay over. And I know it sounds totally freaky, but she's paying me $10,000 to do it.

Okay, stop hyperventilating. I'll explain everything when I get home on Sunday, which should be around 10:30 in the morning. I already paid three months' rent as you can see by the receipt I got from Dominic. And I left some more money here for you. I just didn't want you to worry any more about moving and all that stuff. Anyway, I know you're going to ground me for not telling you about this, but I was afraid you wouldn't let me do it and I really wanted to do something to help.

So I'll see you on Sunday morning, and please don't worry, and I love you.

Love,
Julia

Chapter 15

'Where is she?' I demanded, checking my watch for the third time in about thirty seconds. It was still 12:05, just like it had been the last two times I'd looked at my wrist. 'How can she be late?'

'Carina, calm down,' Ingrid said, taking a drag on her cigarette. 'Just because no one's ever made you wait before in your life—'

'Please! That's not what this is about,' I said, even though it probably sort of was. No one else had ever dared be late to see me or my family. 'I'm just . . .'

'Nervous about meeting Ribbit?' Ingrid supplied.

I held my breath. 'Basically, yes,' I said.

'Don't worry about it,' Ingrid said. She stubbed out her cigarette in the ashtray on my desk, picked up a hairbrush, and walked over to me. 'Let's just hope he likes brunettes,' she said, her eyes twinkling as she brushed through my freshly dyed hair.

'Does it look okay?' I asked, the butterflies in my stomach partying like it was New Year's Eve. I hadn't looked in a mirror in at least an hour. It was too weird to see Julia looking back at me.

'You could dye your hair purple and still be beautiful,' she said. 'I hate that.'

I smirked, recalling my Markus thoughts of the night before. I wished I could tell him that I was ditching him tonight to hang out with a grungy punk singer. I would just have loved to see the look on his way-too-handsome face.

Suddenly there was a knock on the door. I grabbed my messenger bag and stood up, my heart pounding. This was it.

'Who's there?' Ingrid called out.

'It's Bill,' B.B. replied in a hoarse whisper.

'Come in!' I said, my voice cracking with excitement.

'She's in the stairwell,' B.B. said when he opened the door. 'I had to bribe a security guard and one of the bell-boys. You're gonna reimburse me, right?'

'You'll get your money,' I said impatiently. 'Bring her in.'

B.B. disappeared, and I looked at Ingrid for a reassuring glance, which she provided. Moments later Julia stepped into the doorway. Her hair had been dyed to my exact shade of blonde.

Instantly all the feelings I'd had the night before came rushing back to me. With her new hair, the resemblance was perfect. If Ingrid had taken a picture of her right at that second, I wasn't sure *I* would have been able to tell the difference.

I couldn't believe this girl was able to pull this off. The first time I'd seen her, she had just screamed 'cave dweller'.

And now . . . she was me. I turned away from her and finally looked in a mirror. When I saw my reflection, I swallowed back a lump in my throat. She was me, and I was her.

'Hey . . .' Julia said, stepping uncertainly into the room. She was probably recalling my massive breakdown and wondering if I was about to have another. 'You look so . . . different.'

She placed the box that held my gown down on the bed and walked over to me. Together we looked at ourselves in the mirror. My heart was slamming against my rib cage. Maybe this wasn't such a good idea.

Suddenly I found myself wishing my mother were there – that she would walk into the room at that moment and come right over to me and give me a huge hug. I wanted to prove that Julia and I were still . . . Julia and I.

'Carina,' Ingrid said, snapping me out of my thoughts. 'The Toadmuffin roadie is gonna meet you behind the embassy in fifteen minutes. You better move your butt or you're gonna miss him.' We'd decided on the pick-up spot because all the reporters would be at the hotel and they might have noticed me hanging out conspicuously waiting for someone. The embassy was the only landmark we knew within a few blocks' radius.

I looked at Julia's reflection and she smiled. 'Don't worry,' she said. 'I know what I'm doing.'

Why didn't that make me feel better?

'Carina! Come on!' Ingrid said.

Well, there was no turning back now. I threw my bag over my shoulder, gave Ingrid a quick hug, and headed for the door. Soon I would be meeting Ribbit and everything would be perfect. I had nothing to worry about.

'Good luck!' Julia called out.

For some reason, I couldn't bring myself to say, 'You too.'

'Take the stairwell down a few floors and then get on the elevator,' B.B. instructed me as I stepped into the hallway. 'There are reporters downstairs and they'll notice if the elevator comes down from the penthouse.'

I could always count on B.B. for sneaking advice. 'Thanks,' I said. I pushed open the heavy door to the stairwell, walked down to the tenth floor, then took the elevator the rest of the way. A couple with two daughters got on at the fifth floor and I froze for a moment, waiting for someone to recognise me, but they didn't even give me a second glance.

Not all *Americans know you,* I reminded myself. Of course, the way I looked right then, the residents of Vineland might not even have recognised me. *Which is a good thing,* I told myself.

We all stepped out of the elevator in the lobby and walked right past a little klatch of reporters and photographers. Again, not a second glance. Huh. This was kind of . . . freeing.

Out on the sidewalk I took a left and headed for the embassy, which was only a few blocks away. The sun shone on my face and the traffic rushed by and I realised that I was actually walking by myself. No Ingrid. No Killroy. No security detail. I was completely and totally alone.

Completely and totally independent.

I felt a smile stretch across my face as I stopped at a Don't Walk sign with a group of tourists. I was just one of them. One of a bunch of *regular* people. Suddenly a horn honked and I looked up to see a Jeep full of guys – shirtless guys – speeding by.

'Hey, baby!' one of them called out. 'Looking hot!'

My face reddened, but I laughed. In Vineland no one would ever have dared to say such a thing to me. I'd been told all my life I was beautiful, but I'd never had a guy my age call me *hot*. Was this what it was like for normal teenage girls?

The sign changed to Walk and I scurried across the street with the rest of the crowd. All the way to the embassy I held my head high, looked people in the face, and was recognised by absolutely no one. I was living a dream.

When I reached the embassy, I looked up at the Vineland flag waving in the breeze. How many times had I entered that building this week, surrounded by reporters and protected by bodyguards? If I walked up there right now, the men stationed at the door would probably make me walk through the metal detector!

I giggled and made my way around to the back of the building. It was a nondescript street with a few cars parked along the kerb and a few palm trees shading the sidewalk. As I stood there waiting for Ribbit's roadie, I could barely contain my excitement. I was practically bouncing up and down in my new Skechers and giggling every so often. If anyone had seen me, they probably would have thought I'd escaped from the nearest mental ward.

Suddenly a big, beat-up van squealed to a stop in front of me, its engine rumbling. The passenger-side door swung open with a loud creak and for a split second I had the terrifying thought that I was about to be kidnapped. Then a burly guy with long, frizzy blond hair sticking out from under a bandanna leaned over from behind the steering wheel.

'Julia?' he shouted over the loud music blaring from the van.

'Um . . . yes?' I said, baffled.

'Get in, dude!' he said. His T-shirt read I Brake for Boobs.

This could not be my driver. 'Are you . . . Ribbit's roadie?' I asked.

He let out a loud laugh and shrugged. 'This week I am. Last week I was Dave Navarro's and the week before that I was working for Sum 41.' He reached out a callous-covered hand with a tattoo of a spider on the back of it. 'I'm Crazy Dave.'

Did he really think I was going to shake his hand? God only knew where that thing had been.

'You're kidding me,' I said, looking at the dents in the side of the van. My parents would have keeled over at the thought of me riding in this . . . monstrosity.

'Nope, Crazy Dave's the name,' he said with a laugh. At least he pulled back his hand. 'It kind of stuck after the time I put my head through a bar window after an Alice in Chains concert.'

'No . . . I mean . . . you have to be kidding me with this van,' I said. 'It can't be safe.'

'Safe as kittens,' he said. Whatever that meant. 'Come on. Even Cinderella had to ride in a tomato.'

'A pumpkin.'

'Really?'

'Forget it.' I started walking away.

'Suit yourself,' he said.

He reached over to close the door and I paused. Where did I think I was going? Back to the hotel? Where there already was a Carina? There is such a thing as too much princess.

Crazy Dave had started his van, and it was rattling behind me. I turned around and looked at him through the dirty windshield. He smiled and I clenched my jaw, determined.

'Change your mind?' he asked, leaning out his window.

I sighed. 'I have no choice, I guess.'

'That's what my mother said when the police took me back home,' Crazy Dave said. 'Get in.' He opened the passenger door again.

I just stood there. I had always wondered what it would be like to ride in the front seat of a car, but I'd always thought it would be in a Porsche convertible or a nice Mercedes. You know . . . something in leather. This seat was made out of vinyl and there was a split down the centre that was haemorrhaging foam, although someone had tried to duct-tape it. Another disturbing detail. In the movies they were always using duct tape to cover people's mouths when they were kidnapped.

Don't be such a spoiled brat, I told myself. *You should be happy you have someone to drive you to this concert. And you wanted to be normal, right?*

I closed my eyes, braced myself, and stepped into the van. Crazy Dave hit the gas so fast, the door slammed shut and I was flattened against the back of the seat.

'Where's the seat belt?' I demanded.

He shrugged. 'It's a long story. One day last summer I was cruising down the Pacific Coast Highway, listening to some righteous White Stripes tunes, and what happened was ...'

He spaced out for a second, oddly reminding me of Heinrich the Lisper.

'Actually,' he said thoughtfully. 'I don't think it had seat belts when I bought it.'

'What if we have a wreck?'

He lurched into traffic to a chorus of honks. 'That's crazy talk,' he said. 'I've been crash-free for at least three weeks.'

I gripped the armrest and started silently praying as he stepped on the gas again. Maybe being a normal girl wasn't going to be quite what I had imagined.

Chapter 16

That afternoon was a dizzying swirl. Carina and Ingrid had told me I would be visiting a hospital before the ball, but a few things had been added to the princess's schedule. I ended up having lunch with the mayor of Los Angeles and taking a tour of Bel Aire that included the country club half the girls in my school belonged to. All the while I was being snapped at by Fröken Killjoy to stand up straight and speak with more authority and stop fidgeting with my hair. I was having a hard enough time pulling off the Carina act without her watching every move I made.

And if that wasn't bad enough, we were accompanied by an official Vineland reporter and trailed by at least ten American journalists and photographers. Everywhere I went, people were asking me questions and taking my picture. Even Carina's two bodyguards, Daryl and Theodore, couldn't fend them all off.

By the time we got to the last stop before the hospital, I had a million flashbulb shadows flitting before my eyes, my throat was dry from talking, and my back was killing me from standing up so straight.

'Where are we now?' I asked Ingrid, squinting to see better as we climbed the steps to a dark, serious-looking building.

'It's some old mission,' Ingrid replied. 'I think you're meeting a Buddhist priest.'

'All righty, then,' I said as we walked into the cool, quiet building. What did a Vinelandish princess say to a Buddhist priest, anyway? It sounded like the beginning of a bad joke.

It turned out that the Buddhist priest was in L.A. to lobby for better aid to the children of Bangladesh. I averted my eyes when I shook his hand. He seemed like such a wise, holy man. Could he look at me and tell I was an impostor?

'I appreciate all the aid Vineland has given to poor children all over the world,' he said in a beautiful accent. 'Your country has made the lives of hundreds of thousands of children so much better. We cannot thank you enough.'

He was still gently shaking my hand, and suddenly I realised it was my turn to talk.

'I speak for my country,' I began, amazed at the voice coming out of my mouth – the voice of a princess, 'when I say that we are inspired by your efforts to help the children of the world. Children are our future, and we must continue to work together to help improve their lives.'

About a million flashes went off, blinding me from all directions. I said goodbye to the priest and seconds later we were ushered out of the monastery and into the waiting limo.

'Can't we issue a royal order banning photographers or something?' I asked, shutting my eyes against the purple and red squares floating across my vision.

'You were great!' Ingrid said, grinning. 'You're so natural!'

I glared at her. 'I can't believe I just lied to a Buddhist priest,' I said. 'I am definitely going to hell for all eternity.'

Ingrid rolled her eyes. 'Don't be so dramatic.'

B.B. pulled the limo out into traffic, and on the way to the hospital Ingrid coached me again on how to act once we arrived. I was to listen to everything the doctors told me with a concerned expression and nod as much as possible.

'Carina's pretty good with sick kids, but you don't have to touch any of them if you don't want to,' Ingrid said casually when we stopped in front of the hospital.

'What are you, the Tin Man?' I asked.

Ingrid just looked at me blankly.

'You know, *The Wizard of Oz*? He doesn't have a heart?' I prompted.

'Thanks a lot,' Ingrid said lightly. She was the kind of person who is never insulted by insults. 'I'm not as up on the old movies as Carina is.'

The door to the limo swung open and Killjoy stuck her head inside.

'Girls!' she snapped, causing my pulse to skyrocket. This woman made me more tense with one word than every teacher, boss, and landlord I'd ever had. Combined. 'Let's get going. We're already behind schedule.'

'We're sorry, Fröken Killjoy,' I answered, picking up Carina's purse and stepping out of the car.

The woman drew herself up to her full height, her eyes widening with fury. '*What* did you call me?'

Oh God. What had I done now? 'Uh . . . ,' I faltered. 'Fröken. Kill—'

Ingrid jumped out of the car and smacked my arm. I snapped my mouth shut.

The woman narrowed her eyes at us, then turned and marched towards the hospital. She had the step of the German soldiers I'd seen in old films in history class.

'Isn't that her name?' I whispered to Ingrid.

'No,' she whispered back. 'It's Kill*roy*.'

'Thanks for telling me,' I said, taking a deep breath.

This was going to be a really long night.

We walked into the lobby of the hospital and were greeted by a tall, balding man wearing a white lab coat over a shirt and tie.

'Princess Carina, I'm Doctor Fielding, the chief resident in the children's ward,' he said, reaching for my hand. 'It's an honour to meet you.'

I was about to shake hands with him as I normally would, but then I remembered what Carina had taught me and held out my hand, palm down. He hesitated a moment before grasping my fingers, and I just felt like a total poseur. My simple method of handshaking had thrown this man who spent every day helping sick kids. I wanted to disappear right then and there.

'The honour is all mine,' I said, trying to convey the truth of it with my eyes.

He smiled, and I knew he was comfortable again.

Dr Fielding took us up to the children's ward, where he introduced me to the kids in the playroom. Most of them had degenerative diseases, and he said a few might never leave the hospital. Just looking at their open, tired faces somehow exhausted me.

'Does Carina visit a lot of hospitals?' I asked Ingrid under my breath.

'Like every other day,' she replied.

Wow. Maybe being a princess wasn't all parties and shopping and whirlwind vacations. I noticed a little girl sulking in the corner, playing halfheartedly with a Barbie, and walked up to her.

'Hi,' I said. 'What's your name?'

'Lea,' she replied quickly. She was wearing a San Francisco Giants hat over her bald head.

'Pretty name,' I said. It was the only thing I could think to say.

'Lea is in the hospital for radiation therapy,' Dr Fielding said, stepping up next to me. 'She likes to mess with the nurses – always pushing the button on her bed to call them.'

'Well, that's what the button's for!' Lea said, lifting her little chin.

Dr Fielding laughed. 'Got me there.'

'Are you *really* a princess?' Lea asked me, narrowing her eyes sceptically.

'Yes, I am,' I told her, crouching to the floor.

'Then where's your crown?' she asked, touching my forehead with her fingertip.

'I didn't bring it with me, but I have it down in the car,' I said. Then I had an idea, but I wasn't sure if I could pull it off. It would actually involve giving an order, the idea of which made me cringe. Still, I had a feeling I had a way to cheer the little girl up.

'Daryl?' I said, turning to the security guard, who had

accompanied us into the hospital. 'Would you go down to the car and get my crown? I'd like to prove to this little girl that I really am a princess.'

'Yes, miss,' Daryl said with a little bow. Then he disappeared.

It was almost too easy.

A few minutes later Daryl returned with the black box they transported Carina's tiara in. He placed the box on the little plastic table that was covered with crayons and drawings. I popped open the latches and there was the crown, sitting in a bed of purple velvet.

Lea's whole face lit up. 'Whoa!' she said.

'Do you want to try it on?' I asked.

'Really?' she replied.

'You can wear my hat if I can wear yours,' I said.

She ripped off the baseball cap and tossed it at me like it was a rag. Everyone laughed. I pulled it down over my newly blonde hair, then lifted the tiara and placed it on Lea's head. Her eyes rolled up, trying to see it.

'Here you go,' Dr Fielding said, lifting a small, heart-shaped mirror off the wall.

Lea took one look at her reflection and grinned. She turned her head from side to side and touched the sparkling stones.

'You look better than me,' I told her as flashes popped all around us.

I stood up and we all watched as Lea gave the other girls in the room a turn with the crown. I wasn't sure if Carina would have done the same thing, but I had a feeling I had done the *right* thing.

'She hasn't looked at herself in a mirror since her hair started thinning,' Dr Fielding told me quietly. 'They told me you had a real way with kids. Looks like they were right.'

'Thank you,' I said as Lea did a little spin, showing off for her audience.

I was starting to think that even the hospital visit part of being a princess wasn't so bad. In fact, it was just as amazing as the clothes and the make-up and the jewellery and the hair.

It was just a whole different kind of amazing.

On the way home I couldn't stop thinking about those kids. How was I supposed to be all happy-go-lucky and ballworthy after that? I sat in the back of the limo with the tiara in my lap, staring out the window as we drove back to the posh Beverly Hills hotel Carina and Ingrid were staying in

'You're so much like her it's scary,' Ingrid said suddenly.

'What do you mean?' I asked.

'Whenever we do one of these hospital runs, she's all quiet and moody afterwards,' Ingrid said with a shrug.

'Seriously?' I asked. 'I would think she'd tell B.B. to drive her straight to Rodeo.' I felt uncharitable and icky the second I said it.

'You think she's a complete snob, don't you?' Ingrid asked.

'No!' I answered automatically. Ingrid lowered her chin and levelled me with a dubious stare. 'I mean . . . well . . . she doesn't seem to realise what she has, you know?' I racked my brain for a way to say what I was thinking without insulting her best friend. 'The way she was tossing aside all those clothes those designers had sent her the other day? One of those dresses is worth more than my tuition. Seriously.'

'Yeah, but that's the way her world has always been,' Ingrid said. 'Do you know she had to sneak her first pair of jeans into the palace? And her parents don't even let her wear them outside her bedroom just in case a reporter happens to be in the house for some reason.'

'So? Who cares about jeans when you can wear whatever else you want?' I asked.

'Trust me. If you couldn't wear jeans, you'd miss them.'

'Okay, fine, but does she have to order people around all the time?' I asked. 'She doesn't even say "please".'

'You didn't either when you asked Daryl to go get Carina's tiara,' Ingrid countered.

I flushed. I had said 'please', hadn't I?

'See? It came naturally to you within one day of people following you around and catering to your every wish,' Ingrid said. 'But you have to understand her life. You were bothered by the reporters and their stupid cameras within one hour. Imagine if you had a posse like that following you around all the time. And whenever she leaves the palace grounds, there are more reporters hiding in the bushes. She can't go anywhere or do anything without being tracked.'

I sat back in my seat and took a deep breath. Okay. So having your every move watched would definitely be less than convenient. And between Fröken Killjoy and Daryl and Theodore and the reporters and, yes, even Ingrid, I hadn't had a moment to myself for the last four hours. I couldn't imagine what it would be like every single day.

No wonder Carina was dying for an afternoon masquerading as a normal, denim-wearing, entourage-free human being.

'All right, so it sucks to be a princess,' I said, half resigned and half sarcastic. 'But I still can't wait to put on that ball gown tonight.'

Ingrid leaned across the car and put her hand on my knee with a mock-serious expression on her face. 'That doesn't make you a bad person.'

We both laughed as the car pulled up in front of the hotel. I felt a little thrill of warmth rush through me. All that was left to do was get ready for the ball. And as worried as I was that I might mess up that night, I had to admit that I was psyched. I was about to have my one and only Cinderella experience.

Chapter 17

Walking into the embassy was like walking into a fairy tale. And not the creepy kind where someone gets eaten by a wolf. Everything and everyone in the building seemed to gleam. The walls were covered with thick wine-coloured velvet drapery, and every gold and brass fixture shone in the twinkling lights of the huge chandeliers. The women were dripping with jewellery, and their gowns put the red carpet at the Oscars to shame. The guests sipped from sparkling champagne glasses, and a five-piece orchestra played classical music just loud enough to be heard over the hushed conversation. It took me a moment to rearrange my expression from one of total amazement to calm indifference. I just hoped no one had noticed my mouth hanging open before I had the chance to correct it.

'Oh! Here comes the duchess of Thames,' Ingrid said under her breath as a huge woman with cleavage everywhere rapidly approached us. 'Ask her how dear, sweet Muffy is.'

My heart thunked, anticipating my first real test.

'Princess Carina!' the woman said, her strong perfume

filling my nostrils. 'What a pleasure to see you again.' She bowed slightly and then took both my hands in hers. 'I trust your parents are well.'

'Yes, thank you,' I replied, glancing at Ingrid. 'And how is dear . . . sweet . . . Muffy?' I tilted my head slightly the way Carina did when she asked a question.

The duchess turned pink with pleasure. 'Oh, what a dear you are, remembering my poor little dog!' she said. 'I'm afraid she has a bit of the arthritis, but she's otherwise fine.' She smiled, seeming truly touched by my question. 'Well, I won't keep you. I'm sure you have hundreds of people waiting for you.'

Hundreds? I thought, swallowing hard and hoping my sudden spike in body heat wasn't visible anywhere on my body. *I have to do this hundreds of times?*

'Thank you,' I told the duchess. 'It was nice to see you again.'

Ingrid hooked her arm through mine and led me across the room. 'That was perfect,' she said. 'You might not need me after all.'

'If you leave me, I'll kill you,' I replied. Ingrid laughed and whacked me on the back – hard.

'You're stuck with me for the night. Don't worry.'

Fröken Killroy stood across the room, talking with a distinguished-looking man in a tuxedo. She laughed and brought her hand to her chest, and I suddenly realised she was actually *flirting* with the man. Well, that was good. Maybe he would keep her occupied all night. I was less concerned about messing up in front of random dignitaries than I was about messing up in front of her.

A few people came up to Ingrid and me and introduced themselves, and a waiter offered us champagne, which Ingrid grabbed and I quickly refused. Obviously I needed to keep my head clear.

Finally the two double doors next to us opened and a waiter in a white tux stepped into the room. 'Ladies and gentlemen! Dinner is now served!' he announced.

'Perfect,' Ingrid said as the crowd started to move towards the doors. 'Now you'll just have to make small talk with the people at our table for a while.'

'And remember which forks to use when and to keep my elbows off the table and sit up straight and blah, blah, blah,' I said.

Ingrid smirked at me. 'A princess never says "blah".'

Somehow I made it through dinner with no major disasters. Probably because I barely ate a thing. The first course was some kind of fancy avocado crab salad that I couldn't eat because I was allergic to avocados. But I was glad about that because it was arranged in such a complex tower that I had no idea how to start trying to politely pick it apart. Then came the escargot, which you couldn't have *paid* me to eat. Ironic, considering I *was* technically getting paid to eat it, but oh, well.

I had a little bit of my filet mignon, but I bit into a piece of fat and it took me way too long to get up the guts to secretly spit it into my napkin. After that, I was too nervous to eat anything else.

At least the people at our table were easy to talk to. We were sitting with the duke and duchess of Neandar and their daughter and son, Vivian and Victor. Vivian was a student at Yale, and Victor went to boarding school in Massachusetts. They were practically as American as I was.

'So, what do you think of L.A.?' Vivian asked me as I was trying hard to eat my cheesecake dessert like a princess and not shove half of it in my mouth at one time. I was kind of starving.

'Oh, I love it,' I replied automatically. 'Although I actually want to go back east for school, like you.'

Ingrid kicked my ankle under the table and I had to concentrate to keep from wincing.

'Really?' Vivian replied, looking at her parents with surprise. 'I thought the king and queen were avidly opposed to the American education system.'

I looked at Ingrid, flustered. So that was what the kick was for. 'Oh, well, we're still . . . discussing it,' I said.

Vivian's father laughed, his moustache twitching. 'You keep at it, young lady,' he said. 'I've known your father all my life. He may put up a good fight, but inside he's an old softy.'

The other people at the table laughed politely and I sighed, relieved, and started to slump back in my chair. But Ingrid slipped her hand behind me and pressed my spine, making me sit up straight. I bolted up again and smiled a thank-you to her. She just sipped her water like nothing was going on.

Then suddenly her eyes widened and she brought her glass down, clipping the edge of her plate noisily and almost spilling water everywhere. I followed her gaze to see what had her so freaked and what I saw made my heart skip a beat.

Markus Ingvaldsson had just walked into the room. I had never seen anyone so . . . perfect looking in my life.

Okay, you're supposed to avoid this guy. You're supposed to totally spurn him. You're not supposed to get all gushy about him, I reminded myself.

'There he is, the egomeister himself,' Ingrid said. She lifted her napkin from her lap and folded and refolded it, stealing glances at Markus as he started to work the room, going from table to table to greet people. 'He's probably late because his personal groomers couldn't get his hair right.'

'Seriously,' I said. 'Look at that guy.' Markus stopped to talk to an elderly man, listening intently with his hand poised under his chin and his brow furrowed. It was an obvious pose – completely fake. And when he broke out into a laugh a moment later, it was a big, loud, head-tipped-back kind of laugh. The kind you force out when you haven't been listening to a word the person was saying but have instead been stealing glances at your reflection in the surrounding windows.

'Ugh. He's so in love with himself,' Ingrid said. 'Here he comes.' She sat up straight and fiddled with her silverware, then folded her hands in her lap.

'Ingrid, Carina!' Markus said as he approached us. 'It's so good to see some familiar faces.'

There was a looooooonnnng pause. Every set of eyes in the room seemed to be trained on me. And I couldn't help noticing that Markus smelled really, *really* good.

'Hello, Markus,' I said finally.

He hovered by my chair, and suddenly I realised he

was waiting for me to stand and shake his hand or kiss him or something. Well, he could wait all he wanted. Carina wanted me to give him the cold shoulder, and that was what I was going to do.

'Carina . . . they're adjourning to the ballroom,' Markus said. 'Would you do me the honour of the first dance?'

Ingrid looked at me. The duke and duchess looked at me. Vivian and Victor looked at me. I couldn't take it. This was just way too awkward. I was making an idiot of myself. There was no way Carina would turn him down in front of all these people, would she?

'Um . . . I mean, of course,' I told him, standing up. I heard Ingrid sigh beside me, but I didn't know what else to do. I couldn't imagine, after everything she had told me about Carina keeping up appearances, that she would turn Markus down flat in front of everyone. Princesses didn't do that kind of thing.

Markus looked at me uncertainly for a moment, then smiled and offered his arm. As he led me into the ball-room, I looked everywhere but at him. I did my best to send him the iciest vibes I could. Maybe I would dance with him, but I wasn't going to enjoy it.

Chapter 18

Outside the back door of the club where Toadmuffin was performing, at least twenty girls were begging this huge guy with devil horns tattooed on his big bald head to let them in. Crazy Dave and I walked right through the crowd, and Mr Huge opened the door for us. I smiled at the whining girls as the door closed behind us. Too bad for them.

'Ribbit told me to bring you straight to the dressing room,' Crazy Dave told me. 'Follow me.'

The walls of the club were vibrating with the bass from the music that was pumping out front. Crazy Dave led me down a skinny staircase that was all but pitch-black. A sour, acrid smell filled the air, and I covered my mouth with one hand while feeling along the wall with the other to keep from plummeting in the darkness. My hand ran across something slimy and I jerked it away.

'There you go,' Crazy Dave said, gesturing to a door that was covered in garish stickers screaming band names like Hazy Daze, the Bong Babes, and Woofie and the Chew Toys. There was a smashed beer bottle on the floor in front of it and some kind of still-growing puddle near my feet. Crazy Dave turned towards the stairs again.

'You're not really going to leave me here alone, are you?' I asked.

He snickered. 'Just knock.'

I took a deep breath, winced at the smell again, and stepped over the puddle. When I reached the door, I could hear laughter, guitar strumming, and conversation coming from inside. I smiled slowly. This was it. I was about to meet my rock star.

I knocked on the door.

'It's open!' someone shouted.

Touching the dirty doorknob with only my fingertips, I turned it and walked in. The room was filled with so much bluish smoke I could barely see through it. A guy with pink hair sat on the couch, asleep with a cigarette hanging out of his mouth. Two more guys looked up from their guitars. When they saw me standing there, they just stared.

'Who the hell're you?' one of them said.

All the little hairs on the back of my neck stood on end. No one addressed me like that! But then I realised I wasn't me tonight. People probably talked to Julia like that all the time.

'I'm looking for Ribbit,' I said. 'He's expecting me.'

Then I heard a toilet flush and a door across the room opened. Suddenly I was looking into Ribbit's amazing green eyes and nothing else mattered. Not the smoke, not the smell, not the weird stain on my fingertips from the wall. Ribbit took one look at me and smiled.

'Julia?' he said.

Not even my real name. The love of my life didn't even know me by my real name.

It doesn't matter, I told myself. *You're here!*

'Yeah,' I said. 'It's me.'

'Too cool!' he said, grinning as he looked me up and down.

He crossed the room in two huge steps and wrapped me up in his arms. He was wearing a well-worn black T-shirt and his curly brown hair was pulled back in a messy ponytail. He smelled of sweat and smoke and something sugary – everything a rock star *should* smell like. And suddenly I felt like I was coming home. This was the life I was meant to lead – too-cool girlfriend of a famous rock star, not pampered princess of Vineland.

When he pulled back, he looked into my eyes and smiled again. 'Come on,' he said. 'Our set's about to start.' He looked over his shoulder at his band mates and hitched up the side of his baggy jeans. 'Dudes, some-body's gotta wake up Frodo.'

'I'm on it,' one of them said.

Then Ribbit took my hand and led me back up the stairs. 'It's so cool that you're here!' he shouted over the music as we walked down a narrow hallway. 'My interna-tional e-mail girl!'

He pulled me through a doorway, and suddenly I realised I was on the outskirts of the stage. I could see a sliver of the audience waiting down below – drinking from bottles, bang-ing their heads to the music. A couple of shirtless guys sprayed beer all over each other and growled towards the ceiling, then smacked their heads together. A few of the girls

140

next to them shielded themselves from the spray.

'I'll be watching the show from up here,' I said, suddenly unsure whether I could handle *all* the perks of being a regular girl.

'Yeah, of course, babe!' Ribbit said. His hair hung around his perfect face as he smiled at me shyly. 'If you let me kiss you.'

My breath caught in my throat. In all the time Markus and I had been 'together', he'd only kissed me once. And it had been a short, quick kiss on the lips. I'd always thought he was such a wimp. But now Ribbit's sudden request after knowing me for five seconds caught me off guard.

'Come on, babe,' Ribbit said, lacing his fingers through mine. 'It's me! Ribbit!'

I laughed. Who was being the wimp now? 'Okay,' I said, my heart pounding.

Ribbit leaned forward and kissed me on the lips – a long, slow, lingering kiss. His mouth tasted sweet and I felt my eyes flutter closed. I couldn't have imagined a more perfect first kiss if I'd imagined it every day for a year – which I had.

When he leaned back, I searched for something perfect to say. After all, we were going to remember this moment for ever, right?

'Thanks, sweet lips!' Ribbit said with a laugh. Then he smacked me right on my butt.

And then out of nowhere I had this sudden intense urge to slap him back, right across his face. But before I could even move, he ran out onto the stage and the crowd went insane with cheers. The other three band members rushed

141

out and started the first song – 'Beat 'Em Down' – and the noise was louder than anything I'd ever experienced.

Okay, calm yourself, I thought, struggling for breath. *He's a rock star. He's got a different way of doing things. At least he's not boring and repressed like Markus.*

Suddenly all the girls who'd been hanging around the door earlier surrounded me, screaming and dancing to the music. I looked up to find Crazy Dave ushering the last of them into the little crowd. Before I could think about it, I reached out and grabbed his sleeve.

'Oh! Hey, drivin' buddy,' he said with an easy smile.

'Who are all these girls?' I asked.

'They're Ribbit's other babes,' he replied. My face instantly fell. Ribbit's *other* babes? But this night was supposed to be special. It was supposed to be the culmination of a year's worth of romantic e-mails. Was I just another chick in the crowd to Ribbit? And had every last girl here kissed him for a right to stand in the wings?

'Aw, don't worry,' Crazy Dave said. He leaned in close to my ear and said, 'You're the only one that got to see the dressing room.' Then he grinned and winked at me before lumbering off.

I turned and looked at Ribbit as he bounced around on-stage. *I got to see the dressing room,* I thought. *Lucky me.*

Chapter 19

'You're not yourself tonight.'

Tell me about it, I thought, looking up into Markus's eyes briefly. The second my gaze met his, I had to look away. I kept telling myself he was an egotistical, snobbish jerk, but there was a problem. All Markus had done since we'd started this stupid waltz was ask me how my time in L.A. had been. Asked me about my family. (Well, Carina's family.) Asked me detailed questions and listened to the answers. What kind of egotistical, snobbish jerk did that?

'I suppose I'm a bit tired,' I said.

'Me too,' Markus replied with a smile. 'My father dragged me all over the city today, looking for an estate worthy of the Ingvaldsson clan.'

Okay, now that was a bit more like he's supposed to sound, I thought. Only there was something in the way he said it. Something mocking.

'You're buying a home here?' I asked as we spun around the dance floor. I had to concentrate hard not to look at my feet. At least Markus was doing a good job of leading. I'd only stepped on him twice.

'My father is,' he replied. 'And from the size of the places he was looking at, it's going to be more like a small country than a home. Whatever happened to less is more?'

That *definitely* didn't sound snobby.

'I know what you mean,' I said. 'This dress seemed perfect this afternoon, but carrying all this material around is starting to break my back.'

Markus laughed and I flushed. Oh God. That was such an un-Carina thing to say. And then, to make it worse, I stepped on his foot again.

'Oops! I'm so sorry!' I said with a gasp.

'No harm, no foul,' Markus replied. He gripped my elbows firmly but somehow still politely. 'Maybe we should get off this dance floor. I think we could both use a break.'

Sounds like a plan, I thought. 'I agree,' I said. He led me off the dance floor towards the wall and I saw Fröken Killroy follow us with her eyes. Sheesh! Couldn't I get one second out from under the microscope?

'Would you like to go out on the verandah?' Markus asked.

It sounded like perfection to me. A little air, a little time away from Killjoy's eyes of steel. But then Ingrid twirled by me in Victor's arms and shot me a glare. I was supposed to be hating this guy, not going out on the verandah with him.

'I don't know . . .' I said uncertainly.

'Come on, Carina,' Markus said, his blue eyes sparkling. 'We're old friends. I doubt even Fröken Killroy would think it was inappropriate.'

Wow. It had never even occurred to me that it might be *inappropriate*. Was that the kind of world Carina lived in? One where you couldn't even talk to a guy alone in a public place?

'Shall we?' he asked, raising one eyebrow and offering me his arm again.

My heart skipped a beat when he looked at me like that. All fun and familiar and teasing and direct. He had been doing that all night, actually. Not only was it getting harder for me to find anything wrong with him, it was getting hard for me not to like this guy.

'We shall,' I replied with a small laugh, hooking my arm through his.

The verandah overlooked a beautiful section of Beverly Hills – all winding drives and stucco roofs and orange tree groves. We could see the cars flying by on the highways below and the moon shimmering low in the sky. I took a deep breath and let it out slowly, enjoying the moment of silence, away from the watchful gazes that had crowded the ballroom.

'It's a beautiful city, isn't it?' Markus asked, leaning his elbows on the railing.

'Parts of it are,' I said.

'What parts of it aren't?' Markus asked.

'The part that I . . .' I was about to say, 'I live in,' but I caught myself in time.

'The part that I visited this afternoon,' I told him. 'It was very run down. All graffitied and dirty, with houses in . . . disrepair.'

'Every city has those parts,' Markus said, gazing at

me. 'All we can do is try to find a way to make them better.'

I smiled. It was so simple for him. 'Is that what you're going to do when you take your ministry position?' I asked.

'*If* I take it,' he replied. He looked off across the city again, the muscles in his jaw clenching.

'What do you mean, if?' I asked, curious.

He pushed himself up and looked at me like he was gauging whether or not he could trust me. I looked back at him, surprised. He and Carina had known each other their whole lives. Didn't he trust her?

'You can tell me,' I said. 'You look like you . . . need to talk.'

Markus let out a sigh and gazed at the ground, knocking the tile with his toe a couple of times. 'It's that obvious, huh?' he asked. When he looked up again, his face was full of fear, like he was about to bungee jump for the first time. 'I don't want to be a minister of anything,' he said quickly. 'I want to go to architecture school.'

'Really?' I blurted. Then I pressed my lips together, embarrassed over my shock. But I couldn't help it. Here I'd thought I was talking to a guy who was living off the family name and loving it. I was surprised he had any real interests of his own.

Markus laughed. 'You *really* aren't yourself tonight,' he said.

I smiled. 'I'll take that as a compliment,' I replied.

He watched me for a moment and I felt myself start to blush under his gaze. Inside, the music continued to rise and fall, and women in colourful gowns twirled and laughed and flirted. Somewhere in there Fröken Killroy was probably timing us with a stopwatch.

'Hey,' Markus said suddenly. 'You wanna get out of here?'

'So much,' I said automatically. 'But won't we get in trouble?'

'They'll never even notice we're gone,' Markus said.

I highly doubted that, but I wanted to believe him, so I tried to. Besides, he had this mischievous look in his eye I couldn't ignore. It made my pulse race.

'Where do you want to go?' I asked.

'Someplace my father would kill me for going,' Markus replied. 'I heard about this eatery – this real tourist type of place – Roscoe's Chicken and Waffles?'

My nearly empty stomach grumbled.

'Oh! I love that—'

Damn!

'I mean, it sounds fun,' I said with a grin.

Markus reached out his hand to me. There my heart went again, skipping away. 'Let's go.'

Half an hour later Markus and I were sitting in the front seat of the gorgeous green convertible he'd rented for his trip, munching on fried chicken and using about a thousand napkins. I held my hands as far away from Carina's dress as possible.

'Wow. Hungry?' Markus asked as I dumped another leg bone into the bag we were using for garbage.

'I barely ate a thing at dinner,' I replied.

'Good. It left you more room for the best chicken ever,' Markus replied matter-of-factly.

'Absolutely,' I replied. I sucked the grease off my finger-tips one by one.

'Princess Carina!' Markus said, feigning shock. 'What would the queen say?'

Even though he was kidding, my heart stopped. Since leaving the embassy, I'd let my guard down more than a few times. It was almost too easy out here in my own city, showing Markus around. But I had to keep up the charade. Markus still thought I was someone else.

The fun we were having together . . . he was having it with someone else.

'You're right,' I said, shifting in my seat. 'I should use my napkin.'

An uncomfortable silence filled the car as I wiped my hands. Suddenly I hated myself. I hated this night. I hated everything I was doing. And I was doing it all wrong, too. I was supposed to be alienating Markus so that Carina wouldn't have to hang out with him all the time. And instead here I was running off with him, sitting in a parked car alone with him . . . getting heart palpitations whenever he looked at me.

Carina is going to kill me, I thought, *if Ingrid or Killjoy doesn't do it first.*

'Carina, I was just kidding,' Markus said. 'I didn't mean to upset you.'

'I . . . I know,' I replied. 'I just—'

'Do you miss your mom?' Markus asked gently. 'I know your grandmother's sick. I—'

'Can we talk about something else?' I interrupted. The more he spoke about 'my' family, the more on edge I felt.

I was starting to hate being reminded of what I was doing here. Sitting alone with Markus like this felt more like a lie than anything else I'd done all day. Going to all those events had just felt like putting on a show, but now it was getting . . . personal.

'Okay, what do you want to talk about?' Markus asked.

What's safe? I wondered, trying to think. It wasn't like I could tell him anything about myself. So that left . . .

'Tell me more about this architecture thing,' I said, turning to face him again. 'Where do you want to go to school?'

Markus crumpled up his napkin and shoved it into our garbage bag, then stuffed the whole thing behind his seat. He turned, bringing his knee up onto his seat, and leaned back against the door.

'Okay, but this stays between us,' he said.

'Scout's honour,' I replied.

'What?' he asked.

My stomach dropped. 'Just an L.A. phrase I picked up.'

'Ah,' he said. 'Well, I've always loved architecture, ever since I was a kid. Remember how I was always playing with blocks and Lego and Tinkertoys?'

'Mm-hmm,' I lied.

'Well, after that I moved on to forts and then clubhouses, and then every Christmas I started asking for books on architecture,' he said, growing more animated. 'My dad indulged me because he thought it was just a hobby, but when I told him I wanted to study it, he basically blew up.'

'Really? Why?' I asked. 'Architecture is a good profession.'

'But it's not his profession,' Markus said, his eyes hardening. He wrapped his shoelace around and around his finger. 'You know a little something about expectations, Carina. You know how it is.'

The tone in his voice was suddenly so defeated. I *didn't* know how it was, exactly, but I was starting to understand. His voice made me feel the exact same way I felt every time another past-due notice came to the apartment. Like there was absolutely nothing I could do.

'Have you tried talking to him again?' I asked.

'Not yet, but I'm going to,' Markus said. 'I think.'

He laughed and looked at me out of the corner of his eye. I smiled in response. I knew it was going to take a lot of courage for him to bring it up with his father again, but somehow I believed he would. Markus didn't seem like the type to back down from a challenge.

'I guess we should go back to the ball,' he said, reaching for the keys and starting the car.

I would have given up the ball and the dress and everything else just to hang out in the car with him for another fifteen minutes, but I didn't protest. I knew the night had to end sometime. And I was sure Fröken Killroy was just waiting back at the ball to scream her head off at me.

Markus parked behind the embassy and we snuck in through the back door, through the kitchen and dining room and into the ballroom. I held my breath as we walked around the outskirts of the crowd, approaching Fröken Killroy and her distinguished gentleman. But when she saw me, she simply smiled in an approving way. She must have been really smitten with her new boyfriend.

Moments later Markus and I were back on the verandah where our evening had begun.

'See? We didn't get in any trouble at all,' he said, laying his hand over mine on the railing.

As soon as he touched me, a warm thrill ran up my arm and down through my entire body.

Actually, I thought, *I'm not so sure about that.*

Chapter 20

'Excuse me!' I shouted as I attempted to weave my way through the crowded club, desperately trying to find Ribbit in all the madness. 'Excuse me! Hey! Excuse me!'

The girl in front of me shot me a look that could have killed a small rodent, then moved about an inch to the left. I glared right back at her, then elbowed her in the back as I mashed myself between her and the large guy to my right.

If that girl knew who I was, a little voice in my brain began indignantly. But I stopped myself midthought. Because if that girl knew who I was, she'd probably be totally unimpressed. Most of the people in this place seemed to be unfazed by anything, whether it was three guys with spikes coming out of their faces getting into a fistfight over the last beer or a stranger vomiting on their shoes.

I have to get out of here, I thought, starting to hyperventilate in the middle of the smoky, sweaty, gyrating crowd. I was starting to miss my security detail. If they'd been here, they would have formed a protective barrier around me at all times.

I stood on my toes and craned my neck, looking for

the door. When I finally spotted it, I saw none other than Ribbit himself pushing through it with his band mates.

'Ribbit!' I shouted, shoving through the crowd without bothering to excuse myself any more. I'd made skin-to-skin contact with more people that night than in the rest of my life combined. 'Ribbit! Wait!'

I was finally squeezed free of the club and out into the fresh air. I took a second to get my bearings and take a deep breath. Who knew what a luxury oxygen was? Then I saw Ribbit and his friends climbing onto a bus across the parking lot.

'Ribbit! Wait!' I called, scurrying across the grainy, hole-peppered asphalt.

Ribbit paused in the middle of the steps and spotted me. 'Hey!' he called out, shoving by a couple of drunken girls who were trying to get on the bus. 'Where have you been? I been lookin' all over for ya!'

Really? And where exactly *were you looking?* I thought. But I said, 'You have?'

'Yeah! I thought we were gonna party, but after my set you disappeared,' Ribbit said, hooking his arm around my neck. He started walking us both towards the bus again.

'That was probably when I was on the ten-mile-long line for the bathroom,' I said. 'And I use the term *bathroom* loosely.' I had needed at least three tons of toilet paper to cover the seat.

'Sucks to be a girl,' Ribbit said with a chuckle. 'Us guys can go wherever we want! Right, dudes?'

The guys ahead of us who were slowly climbing onto the bus all cheered. A few of them even raised their fists in the air and slapped hands.

'Come on, babe,' Ribbit said, turning around as he climbed the bus steps. He held both my hands and tried to pull me up with him.

'Um . . . where is this bus going?' I asked. It was almost three in the morning. Pretty soon I was going to have to get started for the hotel so I could relieve Julia of her princess duties.

'Nowhere, for now,' Ribbit said. 'We're just gonna stay in the parking lot and throw our own private party.' He gave me a sexy little smile and I felt my heart start to flutter around. Finally I was going to get Ribbit all to myself. Well, on a bus full of people, but still . . .

I smiled and let him pull me up onto the bus. There were a dozen or so people smoking, drinking, playing music, and flipping bottle caps into an empty Chinese food container. Ribbit knocked fists with his band mates as he walked by them, something I'd seen him do a million times in his videos, then pulled me towards the rear of the bus. He slouched into a long vinyl couch against the back wall and looked up at me expectantly.

'Why don't you shut that door?' he asked, lifting his chin at me. 'It's too noisy out there.'

I turned around and saw that there was some kind of handle sticking out from the wall. I yanked at it and struggled with it, finally succeeding in pulling across a flimsy brown door that was made out of something not much thicker than paper.

'Not very effective,' I said sceptically. The noise was just as loud as ever.

'Yeah, but now we have some privacy.' He reached up, grabbed my hand, and basically pulled me down on top of him. My heart hit my throat.

'What are you doing?' I asked.

'Kissing my pen pal,' he said.

Then he reached up and pulled me to him, slipping his hand around the back of my neck. My first thought was to pull away and get control of the situation, but Ribbit was a really good kisser. And the more I kissed him, the more I wanted to keep kissing him. He tasted like beer and I knew he'd had a lot to drink, but it didn't bother me. Actually, the taste was kind of sexy – forbidden.

If my parents knew what I was doing right now, they'd have simultaneous coronaries, I thought.

Something was digging into my side and I realised that I still had my bag slung over my shoulder. I pulled away from Ribbit and sat up.

'Hold on,' I said. 'Just let me get this off.'

I pulled the bag off over my head and dropped it on the floor. When I turned back to Ribbit, all smiles and tender just-kissed lips, he was snoring.

'Ribbit?' I said, thinking he couldn't be all the way asleep – not that fast. 'Ribbit?' I snapped my fingers in front of his face. He only snored louder.

I took a deep breath and checked my watch. I still had a couple of hours left before I *really* had to leave. Maybe Ribbit would wake up and we could have the nice, long heart-to-heart I'd been looking forward to. Maybe we could still have that moment where we'd look into each other's eyes and know we were meant to be.

Just relax, I told myself, leaning back into the couch and listening to the laughter and shouts coming from the front of the bus. I closed my eyes and took a deep breath, just like my yoga instructor, Kirin, told me to do whenever I got stressed. *Just relax and everything will be fine. The night isn't over yet.*

Chapter 21

'Carina! Carina! Wake up! It's Markus!'

I sat straight up in bed when I heard the persistent pounding on my door. Sunlight was streaming through the windows and I blinked against it, completely confused. Where the heck was I? Who was trying to bust down the door?

'Carina! Please! Your guards won't let me in unless you tell them to!'

Omigod! It was Markus! And I was Carina. And I was . . . in my pyjamas!

I jumped out of bed and ran across the room, checking my face in the mirror. I was all sleep-puffy and flushed, and my hair was sticking out in a million directions. But did I look like Carina without all the make-up?

'Carina, please. I know you're mad, but it's going to be all right,' Markus said.

I turned around and looked at the closed door. Mad? What was he talking about? Yeah, I hadn't been thrilled when our amazing kiss last night had been interrupted by a fuming Ingrid, insisting I come back into the ball and demanding to know where I'd been for so long. But it wasn't Marcus's fault that kissing him felt so good I couldn't think of a single other thing I wanted to do with the rest of my life. Maybe he thought I was mad that we'd never got to talk again after Ingrid had dragged me off – that he hadn't said good night before leaving the ball? But it wasn't like he'd known that he'd never see me again . . .

'Carina? Please let me in.'

'One minute!' I called out in Carina's accent. I rushed into the bathroom, wrapped a towel around my insane hair, washed my mouth out with Scope, then rushed to the door.

'Carina, I—'

Markus took one look at me and blushed. He was wearing a pair of pressed khakis and a blue shirt and his hair was still wet from his shower. He looked like perfection and from his stunned expression, I was clearly unappealing.

'I'm sorry,' he said, looking at the floor. 'I didn't realise you weren't dressed.'

I guess a princess never answered the door in her pyjamas. But technically, I was wearing more clothes than I had been at the ball last night, so I couldn't have cared less.

'Don't worry about it,' I said, standing back from the door. 'Come in. What's wrong?'

Markus strode to the centre of the room, then turned to look at me, surprised. 'You mean you haven't seen it yet?' he asked.

'Seen what?' I said, swallowing.

Markus ran a hand over his face, then grabbed the

remote control from on top of the television. The local news popped onto the screen and the anchor was talking beneath a graphic that read ROYALTY KICKS BACK!

Suddenly my stomach started trying to find a way out of my body.

'. . . seems royal balls aren't this princess's particular brand of fun,' the anchor was saying. 'We've acquired these exclusive pictures of Princess Carina of Vineland out on the town last night with a man *reported* to be her boyfriend, Markus Ingvaldsson . . .'

As he spoke, a series of still photographs flicked onto the screen. Me in my ball gown walking out of Roscoe's swinging a bag of fried chicken. Me picking up a newspaper for a man after he'd dropped it on his way in. Me licking my fingers in the front seat of Markus's car, an obscene expression on my face – eyes half closed, lips puckered.

'I think I'm going to throw up,' I said, lowering myself onto the edge of my bed.

'Carina, this is my fault,' Markus said, kneeling in front of me. 'I already took full responsibility with my father, and I'll do the same with your father when I get back to Vineland. I—'

'*Carina!*'

My heart stopped beating as Fröken Killroy and Ingrid burst into Carina's room, still in their pyjamas as well. Killroy was about as red as a person can get without full physical meltdown. Ingrid's face was set like a stone statue and grew even paler when she saw Markus kneeling at my feet. That was when I knew I was done for. If Ingrid wasn't on my side, I had no chance.

'You!' Killjoy said, pointing at Markus. 'Get out of her room this instant!'

Markus rose slowly to his feet. 'Fröken Killroy, let me explain—'

'I don't want to hear your excuses,' Fröken Killroy said, getting right in his face. 'You took the princess out of the embassy without security and took her gallivanting around this dangerous city unsupervised. You, Markus Ingvaldsson, should know better.'

Markus actually hung his head.

'I am responsible for this girl and you have made me look like a fool,' Fröken Killroy continued, her voice quivering. 'Now get out of my sight.'

Markus cast one last apologetic look at me, then walked out of the room. The moment he was gone, I felt completely and totally alone. Little did he know that I was never going to see him again. The thought made my stomach clench even more than Killjoy's anger.

I looked at Ingrid again, hoping for an ally, but she crossed her arms over her chest and looked away. How could I blame her? I'd got her best friend in serious trouble by doing the one thing Carina had specifically asked me not to do – hanging out with Markus. Even kissing him.

'You, young lady, will pack your things immediately,' Fröken Killroy told me. I felt like I was shrinking under her kryptonite gaze. 'We are going to be on that three o'clock flight home, and I will tell your parents all about your indiscretion.' She stood up straight and smoothed her robe down. 'I'm sure the moment your parents hear about it, they'll want you there immediately. And they'll probably have my head.'

She turned and swept out of the room. My heart slammed against my rib cage as I stood shakily.

'Ingrid, I—'

'I can't believe you did this to Carina,' Ingrid said harshly. 'All you had to do was follow a few simple instructions. No. *One* simple instruction. *Stay away from Markus!* How hard could it be?'

Extremely, I thought.

Ingrid's face was all red and blotchy and her eyes were brimming with tears. Suddenly I felt like someone had smacked me upside the head. The Ingrid I'd known for the past few days would have thought this whole thing was hilarious. These weren't tears of sympathy for her friend. She was crying because she felt betrayed. She was crying because – wait, was it possible? She was *jealous.*

'Oh my God,' I said. 'You like Markus, too.'

'What?' she blurted, her face contorting with disbelief. And then I knew it for sure.

'You do! You were all happy when Carina told me not to talk to him,' I said. 'And the one detail you pounded into my brain a billion times was that I should stay away. And . . . and when he walked into the room last night, your whole face lit up. I thought you were just on edge because of what we were doing, but that wasn't it. You *like* him.'

Ingrid glared at me through glassy eyes for a moment, then took a deep breath and shook her head. 'You know, I was going to help you pack up all Carina's crap, but forget it,' she snapped. 'You can do it yourself.'

She stormed out of the room, slamming the door behind her. I sank down onto the bed, wondering how I could have let things go so wrong in so little time. I'd got Carina in trouble, I'd got Markus in trouble, I'd hurt Ingrid's feelings, and I might have got Fröken Killroy fired.

I'd say that my trial day as a princess had been highly unsuccessful.

Chapter 22

I woke up with a start, and my eyes instantly filled with tears from the harsh sunlight. I squeezed them closed and covered them with my hand, then lifted my head. My neck spasmed painfully.

'Ow!' I cried out, sitting up straight. I rubbed at the pain, but it refused to go away.

What kind of position did I sleep in?

And that was when I felt it. The bumping and rumbling beneath me. The distinct sense of *being in motion*. I opened my eyes and for the first time realised where I was. I was in the back of Ribbit's bus. I had been sleeping with my face on Ribbit's *chest*! And now the bus was . . . moving!

All the blood in my body rushed right to my head and I went into full panic mode. It was bright as day out. All I could see through the windows was dirt. Miles and miles of brown dirt. Where were these people taking me?

'Ribbit! Ribbit! Wake up!' I shouted, shaking him as hard as I could. He blinked a few times without actually opening his eyes and flung his arm over his forehead. 'The bus is moving!' I yelled at him, my voice all screechy.

'It does that sometimes,' he said groggily. Then he rolled over onto his side and started snoring again.

I had never been so angry in my entire life. Not even at Ingrid that time she stole my favourite pair of Jimmy Choos and then kicked one into the lake on the back property when she was trying to imitate *Moulin Rouge*. I glanced at my watch and my heart dropped. It was already 10 a.m. According to our deal, Julia was supposed to be leaving for home right now. Had she done it already? Had she blown my cover?

Oh God. I am going to be under twenty-four-hour surveillance for the rest of my life, I realised.

I stood up and banged my head into a cabinet above me so hard I swear it left a dent. Wincing in pain, I stumbled towards the flimsy door, the movement of the bus causing me to lose my footing more than once, and yanked the paper-thin partition aside.

Everyone on the bus was sleeping. Men lay on top of women. Women drooled on men's shoulders. One guy had fallen asleep face down with his nose stuck between the strings of his guitar, pointing down into the little hole. I stumbled towards the front of the bus and found Crazy Dave at the wheel.

'Dave! You have to stop the bus!'

He looked up at me, startled, and swerved into oncoming traffic. Some guy in a blue car slammed on his horn and veered off the road to avoid us.

'You scared me, little lady,' he said. 'And that's not easy to do.'

'Please, Dave,' I said, trying my best to be patient. 'You have to let me off this thing.'

'I don't think so, Jules,' he replied, shaking his head. 'If I let you off here, one of three things will happen – you'll either die from sun exposure, get eaten by coyotes, or get picked up by a bunch of guys even more indecorous than this crew.'

'Indecorous?'

'Hey. I read.'

I took a deep breath and let it out slowly. 'Okay, then turn the bus around,' I said. 'I have to get back to Los Angeles.'

That got a laugh so loud, the guy with the guitar strings up his nose flinched, letting out a dissonant twang as he yanked his face free.

'That ain't gonna happen,' Crazy Dave said. 'We gotta be in El Paso by tonight. We got a gig.'

'El Paso?' I asked. 'Where's El Paso?'

'It's in Texas, little lady,' Dave said, putting on a Western movie accent.

'Texas?' I said breathlessly, falling into the nearest seat. As a dignitary, I had to be up on my world geography. And I knew Texas very well because that was the state the current president of the United States was from. So I knew too well that Texas was *way* far away from Los Angeles.

Okay, don't panic, I told myself. *You have to call Ingrid. She'll know what to do.*

I opened my messenger bag and dug around in it until I located my cell phone, which, naturally, had turned itself off overnight. Ingrid had probably been trying to call me all morning and if my phone had been on, I would have heard it, and it would have woken me up, and I wouldn't have been in this mess.

I turned the phone on and sure enough, it was flashing like crazy. I had ten new messages. I didn't even bother to listen to them. I quickly dialled the number of Ingrid's suite at the hotel. She picked up on the first ring.

'Carina?' she blurted.

'Ingrid, I am in so much trouble,' I said.

'Where the hell are you?' she demanded.

'I fell asleep on Ribbit's bus and now I'm halfway to Texas,' I told her, scrunching my eyes closed.

'Texas! Where's Texas!?'

'It's nowhere near L.A.,' I replied with a sigh.

'Well, you have to get your butt back here.'

'Like I don't know this,' I said. 'But I'm in the middle of the desert. There's no place for me to get off.'

I could practically hear Ingrid's brain working. 'Okay, tell the driver to let you off in the next town and then pay somebody to drive you back here.'

'Great plan, except I have almost no money,' I said. 'Fröken Killroy gave me a little, but I never got my Vinelandish money exchanged. No one ever makes me pay for myself anyway. '

There was total silence on the other end of the line. Even Ingrid was out of ideas.

Oh God, what had I done? I had betrayed my parents, deceived Fröken Killroy, stolen away from all my security people, and got myself stranded in the desert. And for what? For a few sloppy kisses from a guy who'd passed out on me?

Suddenly I wished Markus were there. If he'd been with me, he'd have taken charge. He'd have made me feel safe. If there was one thing Markus had going for him, it was that he was naturally noble. And smart. And level-headed. Okay, so that was three things he had going for him. That and he would never have slobbered all over me and then fallen asleep.

'Well, how else are we going to get you back here?' Ingrid asked. 'Your flight leaves at three o'clock.'

'Hang on a second,' I told her. I covered the mouth-piece with my palm.

'Dave, how far are we from Los Angeles?' I asked him.

'Few hours,' he said. ''Bout five.'

I swallowed hard, my heart sinking. There was no way I'd make it back in time. I felt my eyes start to well up with tears as I leaned back in my seat. I pinched the top of my nose between two fingers and drew in a shaky breath.

'Ingrid,' I said. 'You're going to have to bring an imposter back to Vineland.'

Chapter 23

'Um . . . Ingrid? Shouldn't *Julia* have called by now?' I asked as nervous sweat cemented my linen dress to my back. I was sitting in the back of Carina's limo with Fröken Killroy's beady little eyes boring a hole through my face. We'd been in the car for twenty minutes and she hadn't blinked. Not even once.

'Don't worry, she will,' Ingrid said, looking down at the screen on her cell phone. Ingrid pressed a few buttons on the phone and I could tell she was typing in a text message. Trying to look as casual as possible, I craned my neck to read the screen.

SHE'S ON HER WAY! SHE'LL BE THERE!

She better be, I thought as Killroy narrowed her eyes at us. I sat back in my seat and looked out the window as the familiar L.A. streets flew by. It was almost three o'clock, and I was still a princess. A very nervous, very guilt-ridden princess, and a majorly high flight risk. Every time B.B. pulled the car to a stop at a red light, I considered jumping out and running for my life. But considering the fact that Carina's security people were following along in the car behind us, I guessed it probably wasn't the best idea.

Just come to the airport, Ingrid had said back at the hotel.
She'll meet us there. She just . . . overslept.

I should have said no. This hadn't been part of our
deal. I was supposed to leave the hotel at 10 a.m. exactly.
But how could I turn Ingrid and Carina down after all the
trouble I'd caused? So I had stupidly agreed and now I was
on my way to LAX, where a charter flight was just waiting
to whisk Carina off to a whole other continent. There was
just a little too big of a risk factor here. If our timing was
even a smidge off, Fröken Killroy was going to expect me
to get on that plane. She'd probably put me in a headlock
and drag me on if she had to.

'Carina,' she snapped. 'Don't slump.'

I sat up straight and smoothed the brim of the black
felt hat Ingrid had made me wear. My hair was all hidden
inside of it so that when we met Carina at the airport, she
could take it and hide her brown hair in it as well and no
one would realise the sudden colour change.

Of course, just touching the hat made me think of my
mother, who was most likely freaking out right about
now. She'd probably found my note, waited until ten-
thirty, when I said I'd be home, and then panicked. She
was probably at the Vineland Embassy right then screaming her head off at the guards.

I was so dead.

The limousine took the off-ramp for LAX and my
palms started to sweat. I kept shooting Ingrid looks, but
she was completely ignoring me. As we pulled up in front
of the terminal, I kept my eyes peeled for Carina – for any

sign of a girl in dark sunglasses and a baseball cap. But she was nowhere to be found.

B.B. opened the door for me, and as I stepped out of the car, I stumbled nervously, right into his arms. I would have given anything to be back home in Venice, safe and sound, in our crappy apartment with my fleabag of a cat and my panicked mother.

As Fröken Killroy gave directions to the porters, Ingrid stepped up beside me and pressed something into my hand. When I saw it was a Vineland passport, my mouth went dry. I opened it and Carina's face smiled back at me.

'What am I supposed to do with this?' I hissed to Ingrid.

'Just give it to the lady behind the counter and she'll hand you your ticket. You can give everything to Carina when she gets here,' she whispered.

I glanced around again, hoping I might have missed her the first time. *Please let her be here. Please!* I thought. *I swear I'll never do anything dishonest again.*

'Princess! Don't dillydally!' Fröken Killroy said, holding open the door for me.

I took a deep breath and stepped into the heavily air-conditioned terminal. The woman behind the counter could barely speak as she handed me my ticket. I looked down at the slip of paper and I swear, it felt like a death sentence.

The second Ingrid stepped away from the counter, I grabbed her arm and pulled her aside from the rest of the delegation.

'Where *is* she?' I demanded.

Ingrid snatched her hand back. 'Look, as soon as she gets here, B.B. is going to honk the horn. Then you say you left something in the car, you two will meet in there, and you'll switch clothes.'

'Fine, but when?' I asked, my heart pounding out of control. 'The plane is supposed to leave in fifteen minutes.'

'Calm yourself,' Ingrid said, completely unsoothingly. 'If you don't stop losing it, someone is going to realise something is up.'

I tried to chill. I really did. But the rest of the delegation was already lining up at the gate. Time was running out. Fast.

'I'm just going to run to the bathroom,' Ingrid said suddenly, glancing past my shoulder. 'I'll be right back.'

Before I could even open my mouth, she'd hurried off. And then I felt a hand come down on my shoulder. My heart was in my mouth.

'Time to go, Carina,' Fröken Killroy said.

'No!' I blurted. 'I . . . Ingrid's in the bathroom!'

'No, she's not! She's right there!' Killroy said, pointing towards the gate. I turned, my stomach heaving, and saw Ingrid cutting the line of security personnel to slip onto the plane. She shot me an apologetic backwards glance.

Oh my God, I thought, my vision going a little blurry. *Carina isn't coming. Ingrid knows she isn't coming. They set me up!*

Fröken Killroy was pulling me towards the gate and I was barely resisting. It was like I suddenly couldn't get control of my muscles. A million thoughts flooded my mind. I was being kidnapped. I was being set up to replace the princess of Vineland. Were they going to make me live out my life impersonating someone else? Had this been the plan from the beginning?

'Carina! What are you doing? Walk like a human being!' Killroy scolded me.

'This . . . this is a mistake!' I heard myself say. 'I don't belong here!'

'And that's exactly why we're taking you home, Your Highness,' some random airline worker said to me with a grin, taking my ticket.

'No! I can't get on that plane!' I said, finally coming to long enough to try to pull away from Killroy.

'Daryl, Theodore – Carina is having another one of her tantrums,' Fröken Killroy said, sounding bored.

Suddenly I was sandwiched in between the two impossibly strong men and basically carried onto the plane, my toes dragging along the floor.

'You people don't understand,' I said, trying for a calm, rational voice but sounding more like I was having a breakdown. 'I'm not Princess Carina. My name is Julia Johnson. I live in L.A.'

'Right. Like the time you bought that ticket to Australia and tried to convince us that Nicole Kidman was your real mother and she wanted you back?' Daryl said sarcastically.

'Or the time we found you sneaking over the wall and you pretended you had delirium from eating bad oysters?' Theodore added, amused.

Wow. Carina really *was* desperate.

The two security guys dropped me in the seat next to Ingrid, who was flipping through a magazine with a bored expression on her face. Daryl even leaned in and belted me into my seat.

'Have a pleasant flight, Your Highness,' he said with a

smirk as the plane started to move away from the gate. Then he walked off towards the back, leaving me alone with Ingrid.

'This is because of Markus, isn't it?' I said to her under my breath. 'You're doing this to me because of Markus.'

'Don't be so dramatic,' Ingrid said. 'You're gonna love Vineland.'

Chapter 24

I sat in the front seat of the bus, watching the screen on my cell, waiting for an update from Ingrid. If she had somehow managed to trick Julia onto the plane to Vineland, she had bought me some time to figure out a plan. If Julia had refused to go and exposed our whole little switch, then there was probably some kind of government agency tracking me down right now.

Finally my phone beeped and a text message scrolled across the screen.

MISSION ACCOMPLISHED! WE'RE TAKING OFF RIGHT NOW! I REALLY AM SOOOOO GOOD!

I let out a little sigh of relief but somehow didn't feel much better. Maybe it was because the desert was still stretching out all around me. Maybe it was because I still had no idea how I was going to get back to L.A. Maybe it was because Crazy Dave had been singing Red Hot Chili Peppers songs at the top of his lungs for the past half hour – badly.

Also, I really had to . . . use the bathroom. And I was *not* going to go in the smelly closet thing in the back of the bus. I had to draw the line somewhere.

Okay, I have to tell them who I am, I thought calmly. *I have no idea how I'm going to prove it, but if they believe me, they'll realise they have to take me back to L.A.*

It was a flimsy plan, I knew. Unfortunately, it was the only plan I had.

I stood up, grabbing the back of my seat as the bus rumbled beneath me, and scanned the seats. I spotted Ribbit sitting towards the back with one of his guitar players, going over some new lyrics. He was wearing a blue T-shirt and his hair was pulled back in a ponytail. Little lines formed above his nose as he concentrated on scribbling something down in the notebook in front of him.

Two days ago the sight of Ribbit in the midst of creating would have made me all giddy and fluttery. Now all I wanted to do was shake him and scream at him for getting me into this mess.

I walked down the centre aisle and paused next to Ribbit. He didn't look up. Not even when I cleared my throat.

'Ribbit, there's something I have to tell you,' I said firmly.

'One sec, babe,' he said, lifting his pencil at me. He scribbled something down about flaming lips and fire extinguishers. *Oh, how very deep.*

'Ribbit, you have to make Dave turn this bus around and take me back to L.A.,' I said. Then I took a deep breath. 'I'm not Julia Johnson. I'm actually Princess Carina of Vineland, and if I don't get back to my country soon, there's going to be serious trouble.'

Ribbit and his guitarist looked up at me, and for one fabulous second I thought they believed me. Their eyes

175

were wide with surprise as they processed what I'd said.

Then they cracked up laughing. At me. I felt my face flame with indignation. I had had about enough of being treated like I was just some . . . some regular girl. I mean, if this was how normal people treated other normal people every day, why did anyone ever leave their homes?

'Please,' Ribbit said finally. 'If you're a princess, what are you doing hanging around with a bunch of losers like us?'

'That's what I'd like to know,' I snapped back.

'You callin' us losers?' the guitarist said, shifting in his seat.

'He did it first!' I pointed out. Ribbit had gone back to his writing, so I crouched to the floor to try to force myself into his line of vision. 'Ribbit, come on, think about it. You *know* I'm from Vineland and you know it was next to impossible for me to get away to come to the concert. And . . . and . . . I always signed my e-mails to you with a *C*, right? *C* for Carina?'

'Never really thought about it,' Ribbit said, not bothering to look up from his notebook.

I let out a frustrated groan and stood. Clearly this was not going to work. And I had nothing in my bag to prove who I was. Julia had my passport. And I was carrying a wad of Vinelandish money, but that only proved I was from Vineland.

I looked around the dingy bus and realised this was my fate. I was going to be stuck with these people until they got to El Paso. But *then* what was I going to do – become a cowboy?

'Pit stop, folks! Let's make it quick!' Crazy Dave shouted suddenly as the bus lurched and slowed. Everyone started to rouse from their seats, stretching and yawning and moaning. I looked out the window and saw a huge building looming up out of the desert like a mirage. There were dozens of trucks and buses and cars parked out front and a large sign on top of the building that read simply, Eat.

I couldn't believe it. I'd thought there was going to be nothing until we got to Texas. But if this was a restaurant, then they had bathrooms. And if they had bathrooms, then at least I could take care of one of my problems. I scurried to the front of the bus, grabbed my bag, and was out of there before anyone else had managed to get up from their seats.

I walked into the building and at least twenty big, burly men in the most stunningly awful array of plaid shirts and tattered baseball caps looked up from the tables. From the expressions on some of their faces you would think they'd never seen a female before. I held my head high and walked up to the counter, where a woman with very large hair and very pink lips was taking someone's order.

'Where's the bathroom?' I asked.

She looked me up and down, then snapped her gum.

'I didn't hear the magic word, sweetie,' she said.

Magic word? What on earth was this woman talking about? Did I have to say 'abracadabra' to magically open the door to the bathroom?

'Uh . . . I think she means "please",' the guy next to me at the counter said.

I shot the guy a glare, then did a quick double take. He was about my age, maybe a little older, with light blond hair and eyes as blue as the protected lakes in Vineland. Just looking at him made me feel homesick.

I cleared my throat and swallowed my pride. I mean, I *really* had to find the bathroom.

'Where's the bathroom, *please*?' I asked.

The woman clicked her tongue at me. 'Round the outside of the building on the left.' Then she pulled out a stack of brown napkins from a holder on the counter. 'You'll need these. We're out of toilet paper.'

I grimaced as I picked up the rough, scratchy napkins. And to think, before I'd come to L.A., I'd thought the United States was the most modern, civilised country in the world. I pushed through the glass door and walked as fast as I could around the side of the building, ducking into the bathroom just as Toadmuffin's drummer was coming out of the men's room. Apparently *they* all knew where the bathroom was.

The stench that hit my nostrils when I closed the door behind me almost made me black out. It was no wonder they were out of toilet paper. The floor of the bathroom was covered with wads of it, along with mud, a couple of sanitary napkin wrappers, and a brown paper bag with some kind of stain on it.

The toilet seat looked like it hadn't been cleaned in a decade.

I want to go home, a little voice in my brain whined. But I knew that wasn't going to happen anytime soon. I was always telling everyone that I could do things on my own. Now was the time to prove it. Luckily there was a container of liquid soap on the sink. Breathing through my mouth to block the overwhelming smell, I squeezed a blob of soap onto one of my napkins and set about washing down the toilet seat, even as my body yelled at me to just forget about germs and go already.

Imagine what Mother and Father would think if they saw me now, I thought, a sudden irrational smile flitting to my lips. *Princess Carina cleaning toilets!*

When I was finally satisfied with the job I'd done, I held my nose and did what I had to do. Then I scrubbed my hands for about five minutes before using a napkin to open the door again.

When I emerged from that disgusting bathroom, I felt about five hundred times better. I felt like I'd accomplished something. Even if all I'd done was cleaned off a toilet seat.

Tossing back my hair, I walked around the restaurant, ready to try one last time with Ribbit. And if it didn't work, then I was El Paso bound. Maybe this place was a big city where I could exchange my money and hire a car back to L.A. Or maybe it even had an airport and I could *fly* back!

Suddenly I felt like I had some options. I felt like everything just might be okay. Then I came around the corner and saw the Toadmuffin bus pulling out of the parking lot, kicking up clouds of dust as it rumbled off.

Everything was definitely *not* okay.

Chapter 25

'In what year was the Queen Ariana Memorial Hospital built?'
Fröken Killroy snapped at me, bringing a whip down on my desk.
I looked up at her, my heart pounding, and saw that her wattle
was hanging lower and lower, making her look like a half woman,
half turkey. She glared at me and her eyes flashed red.

'Baaaaawk,' she said angrily.

'Uh . . . 1898?' I said, cowering in my seat.

'Sit up straight!' she shouted, bringing the whip down again.
'You're a princess!'

Daryl and Theodore appeared out of nowhere and grabbed me
under my arms, pulling me up until my back was ruler straight.

'Name all the dukes and duchesses of Vineland and the
provinces in which they reside! East to west. In height order!'
Fröken Killroy demanded.

'Okay . . . um . . . Duke Charles and Lady Marielle of Glockenshire
. . . uh . . . Duke Michel and Duchess Corinne of . . . of . . .'

I was drawing a blank. I couldn't remember a single province
or the names of the lakes or the year the university was built. I
couldn't remember anything about my country.

Because it's not your country, a voice whispered in my ear.

You don't belong here, and they're going to find you out, and when they do . . .

I looked up and saw Ingrid standing next to me with a smirk on her face. Slowly she drew her finger across her neck.

'You have to let me go home!' I shouted. 'I just want out of here!'

A million royal handlers closed in on me, circling around the desk, their eyes blank like zombies. I was just about to let out a scream when I heard a roar in the distance. The roar of a power-ful engine. Suddenly the crowd of bodyguards split and a pair of headlights emerged in the darkness. A car screeched to a stop right before my desk. A convertible.

'Leave her alone!' a familiar voice shouted.

And then Markus emerged from the car, swinging his legs over the door and pushing through the crowd toward me. He reached out his hand across the desk and smiled, looking right into my eyes.

'Don't worry,' he said. 'You're home.'

I smiled and took his hand, and suddenly we were in his car, cruising up the Pacific Coast Highway, the sun on our faces. And everything just felt . . . right.

'You're home! Carina! Princess Carina! We're here!'

I was suddenly jarred awake to find a stewardess touching my shoulder. I blinked up at her in confusion, wanting to be left alone so I could get back to my dream.

'Welcome home, princess,' she said, standing up straight and folding her hands in front of her. 'Pleasant dreams?'

I turned and looked across Ingrid's now empty seat to the window. It was daylight outside, and past the runway I could see green grass and towering snowcapped mountains.

I couldn't believe it. I really was in Vineland.

'Carina?' Ingrid said, appearing behind the stewardess's shoulder. 'Are you coming?'

I stood up slowly and smoothed down my hair, my pulse already racing. What did Ingrid expect me to do? Was she really going to make me go to the castle and try to convince Carina's parents that I was their daughter? This was insane!

'Would you mind giving me and my friend a moment alone, please?' I asked the stewardess.

'Of course, Your Majesty,' she replied, bowing her head. She disappeared out the side of the plane onto the walkway that led to the gate.

I took a deep breath and looked Ingrid in the eye. She folded her arms over her chest and leaned against the wall. We stood there like that for a moment, staring each other down.

'Ingrid, you have to tell me—'

'Julia, I didn't mean to—'

We both stopped talking. 'You first,' I said.

'Okay,' Ingrid said, standing up straight. 'I'm sorry I tricked you, but Carina basically got lost in your country somewhere and we had to bring someone back to Vineland. You have no idea how much trouble she would be in if her parents found out what we did.'

'Do you have any idea how much trouble *I'm* going to be in when my mother finds out I'm in another country?'

'So your mother will be mad – big deal,' Ingrid said with a shrug. 'Carina's parents will never let her leave the palace again for the rest of her life. Seriously.'

I couldn't believe this. She still didn't care at all about me and how this whole little plot was affecting my family. I couldn't even imagine the condition my mother was in at this point.

'Look, Carina will be here as soon as she can get a flight out of Los Angeles,' Ingrid said. 'I just found out her parents had to go to Sweden today for some funeral, so they won't even be back until the morning. Carina will probably be back by then, so just . . . play along, okay?'

I was about to tell her she could just take her little plan and blow it out her butt. I'd make them give me a blood test, a fingerprint test, a DNA test – whatever. All I wanted to do was prove I wasn't Carina and get the heck home.

'Carina's already in enough trouble as it is,' Ingrid said, picking up her carry-on bag and starting for the door.

A knot of guilt instantly formed in my stomach. She was right. Carina was in major trouble and I was responsible. Maybe I could just keep up the act for one more day. Then it would all be over. I mean, I *had* always wanted to come to Europe . . .

'Carina, the car is waiting,' Fröken Killroy said, appearing at the side door of the plane.

'Coming,' I said, shaking my hair behind my shoulders and pressing my lips together with resolve.

It was time to take responsibility for what I had done. All I could do was hope that Carina had told the truth about her parents – that they were actually around as little as she claimed. Because there was no way they were going to believe I was their daughter. Maybe I could fool the world, but a parent is a whole different story.

*   *   *

Now that we were back 'home', Fröken Killroy allowed Ingrid and me to have the princess's limo to ourselves. We were both silent as the car sped along a pristine highway surrounded by fields filled with grazing cows. The mountains rose towards the sky in the distance and the air was so clean it made me realise that I had been breathing in smog my entire life.

Still, as beautiful as the surroundings were, they could do nothing to lift my spirits. I had never felt so alone. I ached to talk to my mother and let her know that I was okay. I ached for her to hug me and tell me everything was going to be fine.

'Carina, listen,' Ingrid said suddenly, casting her eyes towards the driver. 'Don't tell *Julia* about . . . uh . . . about what you figured out this morning at the hotel, okay?'

I turned and looked at her for the first time since we'd left the airport. She had this vulnerable look on her face that I'd never even imagined Ingrid was capable of.

'You mean about you and—'

'Marrr . . . cellus. Marcellus,' Ingrid answered, looking nervously at the driver again. 'She'd freak if she knew I liked him.'

I glanced at the driver and saw him look at me in the rearview mirror. Apparently someone was always listening.

'But Julia doesn't like Marcellus, does she?' I asked, raising my eyebrows.

Ingrid sighed and pulled her cell phone out of her bag. She typed something into it and then held it out to me.

NO. BUT HE BELONGS TO HER.

My heart twisted in my chest and I nodded slowly.

What had I been thinking, letting myself have feelings for Markus? He was so totally, completely untouchable, it was almost surreal. Leave it to me to get my first serious crush on a guy who lived in another country and *belonged* to someone else. And, oh yeah, didn't even know who I was.

I took a deep breath and let it out slowly. It was time to stop daydreaming about Markus and focus on the task at hand – getting through the rest of this day and night. Soon Carina would be here and I would go back to my normal life. It would be like none of this had ever happened.

We had been driving along a high stone wall for a few minutes now, and the driver suddenly turned the car down a short drive and came to a huge, iron gate that opened instantly. We proceeded along a wide, winding drive bordered by beautiful fir trees. Then we came around a bend, and the castle appeared as if out of thin air.

My breath caught in my throat at the sight of it. The palace seemed to stretch out for miles in either direction, and its towers reached far into the sky. The pale white brick of its walls shone in the sunlight, and a bubbling fountain stood in the centre of the circular drive. I could see rich draperies hanging in each and every window, and red flowers exploded from boxes beneath the lower ones. More red flowers lined the drive, and a pair of horses were tethered to a post near the front door, making me feel like I'd just time-warped back to the nineteenth century.

'Whose horses?' I asked.

'Yours,' Ingrid said, looking at me meaningfully, then glancing at the driver again. 'You have six horses, remember? Jeez, Carina, how long have you been in America?

The grooms were probably just exercising them for you in case you wanted to ride this afternoon.'

Yeah, like that was gonna happen. The closest I'd ever come to riding a horse was the five minutes I'd spent sitting on a pony at a petting zoo when I was in kindergarten. I'd cried and my mother had had to pick me up from school.

The driver parked the car and came around to open the door for me. He offered me his hand and I took it, staring up at the castle in awe as I stood. For the first time in my life I knew what the expression 'it takes your breath away' meant. If I was going to be kidnapped from home, this was definitely the place to be held prisoner.

'I have to call my mom,' I said to Ingrid as she joined me at the side of the car.

'The queen is in Sweden for the night, Your Highness,' the driver told me. 'She's staying at the embassy.'

'Oh – yes – thank you,' I stammered. 'I'll . . . call her there.'

Ingrid hooked her arm through mine and led me into the castle. The foyer was at least three storeys high and polished to the point of glimmering. My entire apartment building could have fit into that one room. An intricate mosaic of the Vineland crest decorated the centre of the floor, and three women in maid's uniforms stood at the double doors across the way.

'Those are your servants. The one on the left is your personal maid, Asha,' Ingrid whispered. 'They'll take you up to your room and help you unpack.'

'Wait! You're leaving me?' I asked desperately as she started to move away.

'I have to go. My parents are expecting me.'

'But . . . what do I *do*?' I hissed, clutching her hand.

'Just . . . stay in your room, use Carina's computer . . . hang out,' Ingrid said. 'Either Carina or I will call you, and if you need me, just tell the operator to dial Ingrid.'

'Ingrid! Don't go!' I begged, my heart pounding. The servants were looking at me like, well, like I was a big, fat fake.

'I'm really sorry, Carina, I have to,' she said, her eyes genuinely apologetic. 'Call me.'

And then she rushed out the door. Practically shaking, I turned to look at my *servants* and tried to smile.

'Hi . . .' I said, tentatively approaching them.

'Your Highness,' they all said at the exact same time, in the exact same way. Then Asha stepped forward.

'How was your trip, miss? I'm sure you'd like to wash up. We've already drawn your bath,' she said with a small smile.

'Uh . . . thank you,' I said. Then I saw the other two girls exchange a glance and remembered how Carina treated the people who worked for her. Well, that was one thing this actress was not going to get right. 'I'd just like to go to my room and . . . rest first, I think.'

I just need a phone, I thought. *Take me to a phone.*

'Of course, miss,' Asha said.

The other maids opened the double doors for us and Asha led me to a huge, plushly carpeted staircase. I followed her up the stairs and then down a long hallway lined with doors. Finally she opened the very last door at the end of the hall and moved aside.

I smiled at her and stepped into Carina's bedroom. It was absolutely huge and totally gorgeous. I mean, there were too many flowers and frills and laces and fringes for my taste, but it was still beautiful. She had a four-poster bed dripping with pink velvet and plump pillows, and there was about a mile of open carpet between her bed and her desk, which held a brand-new flat screen iMac. And a phone.

'Anything else, miss?' Asha asked.

'No, thank you,' I replied. 'I'll be fine.' *I think,* I added silently.

'Ring if you need me,' she replied. Then she shut the door and I was left in silence.

I lunged at the phone. There was no dial tone. I was about to just burst into tears when a voice asked, 'Who would you like to call, Your Highness?'

I blinked, startled. 'Um . . . a number in the United States? California?' I attempted.

'What's the number, please?'

I recited my home phone number and held my breath while the phone rang.

'Hello?' my mother answered, her voice strained.

'Mom?' I said, hot tears springing to my eyes. I had made her sound that way.

'Julia! Where *are* you! Are you okay?'

'Yeah, I'm fine,' I replied. I sat down hard in the desk chair and clutched the phone.

'Oh, thank God you called. What is this note all about? And this money? Where are you?' She sounded so desperate and scared, I barely even recognised her voice.

I looked around at the old-fashioned cream-and-gold wallpaper, the ornately gilded mirror hanging on the far wall, the painting of Carina hanging over her bed that made her look like something out of a Jane Austen book.

'I'm . . . uh . . . I can't tell you that,' I said, closing my eyes. 'But I'm going to be home as soon as I can and I'm *fine*. I swear.'

'Julia Lynn Johnson, you tell me where you are or you are going to be grounded for so long you're gonna need a walker to get down the stairs.'

Okay, she was starting to sound like my mother again. 'Mom, you're just gonna have to trust me,' I said quickly. 'I'm fine and I love you and I'll be home soon.'

And then I did the hardest and probably the stupidest thing ever – I hung up on my mother.

Chapter 26

It took about fifteen minutes for me to realise that Ribbit and Crazy Dave were not coming back for me – that they would probably never even notice I was gone. Dave was, well, crazy – definitely in his own little world. If he did realise I wasn't around any more, he'd probably think he'd made me up. And Ribbit? He was so totally self-centred he hadn't even talked to me all morning until *I'd* come to *him*. If he remembered me at all, he'd probably wonder whatever happened to that psycho who thought she was a princess.

I'd never felt so deflated. Just when I'd been getting used to the idea of going to El Paso and figuring out what to do from there, I was stranded in the middle of nowhere. What was I supposed to do now?

Somehow I made myself walk back into the restaurant. The scent of fresh coffee and frying food hit me right away and my stomach suddenly felt hollow. I hadn't eaten anything since Crazy Dave and I had stopped at that burger place the day before. And I hadn't even eaten much then because I wasn't sure that what they'd given me was actual food. I wondered what I could get to eat with the small amount of American money I had.

I found an empty booth by the window and sat down. The plastic place mat appeared to double as a menu. I looked over the breakfast options and was happy to see that I could get eggs and toast for only two dollars. I dug into my bag and checked in my wallet. I had a twenty-dollar bill along with my Vinelandish cash. Perfect. I would eat first, get my strength back, and then figure out what to do. Unfortunately, I had a feeling the only thing I could do was call my mother and bawl my eyes out and beg her forgiveness. That was something I *really* didn't want to think about. Not before I ate, anyway.

'What can I get you?' the magic-word woman asked, approaching me with a pad and pencil.

'I would like two eggs, poached, and wheat toast . . . and coffee,' I said. She looked down at me expectantly. 'Oh! Please,' I added.

'You're getting good at this,' the woman said sarcastically.

I turned bright red. Oh, what I wouldn't have given to be in Vineland right then. She slipped her pencil behind her ear and started to move away.

'Wait!' I called out.

'Something else?' she asked, turning around.

'Yes . . . would you know how I can get back to L.A. from here?' I asked.

'You're in luck,' the waitress said with a smirk. 'Practically every guy in this place is either headed there or is coming back from there.'

I looked around the restaurant, baffled. Did she really

expect me to ask a perfect stranger for a ride back to Los Angeles? One of these men with their huge guts and brown teeth and severe body odour? Who knew what they would do to me once we were out in the middle of the desert? Hadn't she seen *The Vanishing*? Or *A Time to Kill*? Or even *Road Trip*?

Hmm. Maybe I'd been watching too many movies.

'I—'

'Hey! Any of you boys wanna give this girl a ride to Los Angeles?' the waitress shouted at the top of her lungs.

The entire place exploded with shouts and offers – even a couple of whistles. Men rose from their seats to see past the tables and check me out. The way a couple of them looked at me made me feel even dirtier than that bathroom had. I might as well have been a horse at auction.

'Why did you—'

'Hey! I just thought I could help,' the woman said, obviously trying not to laugh. 'I'll be right back with your eggs.'

As soon as she walked off, I saw a tall man with a beard push himself out of a booth a few tables away. He hitched up his jeans, rolled back his shoulders, and sauntered over to me. My heart started to pound and I turned my face away, looking out the window and hoping he would pass me by. He didn't.

'You lookin' for a ride?' he asked, shoving his hands in the back pockets of his jeans. I was about eye level with his belt buckle – a tarnished brass monstrosity representing some kind of flag. It had a big *X* through it with stars inside the *X*. Was this guy not from the United States?

Why would he wear a replica of a flag for a country that wasn't his own?

'I asked you a question,' the man said, pressing his knuckles into my table and leaning down over me. 'You need a ride or what?' His breath was hot and smelled rancid.

'No. I don't,' I said, my heart pounding with fear. 'Thank you.'

'Then why're you askin' for one?' he asked with a wicked smile.

I opened my mouth, but no sound came out. *I am the princess of Vineland,* I thought. *This person can't hurt me.*

Except I wasn't. Not now. And this person could pretty much do whatever he wanted, and it didn't seem like anyone else was going to notice.

'I—'

'She's with me.'

The guy from the counter with the incredible blue eyes fell into the seat across from me. He dropped a huge backpack down on the table and folded his hands on top of it. He was half the other man's size, but he looked up at him confidently – even a bit mockingly.

'Since when?' the man asked, standing up straight again.

'Since now,' the guy answered firmly. '*I'm* driving her to L.A.'

The two guys stared each other down for what felt like an eternity. My hands were starting to sweat, and I pressed them into my jeans. Silently I hoped that the boy with the backpack would win. I wasn't happy about the idea of getting into a car with anyone I didn't know, but if

I had to choose between these two, I knew who the winner would be.

Finally the huge, scary man blinked. 'Eh, it's not worth it,' he said. Then he sauntered away from the table again and smacked open the door to the restaurant.

'Thank you so much,' I breathed the moment he was gone. It was the first time since I'd arrived in America that anyone had done anything even remotely honourable.

'Not a problem,' the guy replied. 'I'm Glenn.'

'I'm Carina,' I said automatically. Then my heart dropped. I couldn't be walking around telling people my real name. What if he recognised me? What about my reputation? What if he tried to take advantage of—

'Carina, huh? Nice name,' Glenn said, pulling his backpack off the table.

Right. Americans don't grow up with pictures of you in their classrooms and on the cover of every other newspaper, idiot, I thought. I really had to start getting used to this.

My food arrived and my stomach growled loudly. I had never seen anything that looked so scrumptious in my life. Even if the eggs were a bit soggy and the toast was a tiny bit burned.

'So, you really need a ride to L.A.?' he asked, leaning back in his seat.

'Yes,' I replied as I shook some pepper onto my eggs. 'Are you really going there?'

'You bet,' he replied. 'I got a job on a movie set.'

'Really?' I asked, visions of director's chairs and huge lights and enormous sets filling my head. 'Doing what?'

'Oh, you know, just . . . getting coffee and running

errands and stuff like that,' he said with a shrug. 'But ya gotta start somewhere.'

'I suppose,' I said, my heart falling. I actually felt kind of sorry for him. Here he was about to come so close to the most glamorous industry in the world, and he was just going to be someone's servant.

'What does that mean, "I suppose"?' he asked, his beautiful eyes flashing.

'Well, look at you,' I said. 'Hollywood loves your type . . . Heath Ledger, Brad Pitt, Leonardo DiCaprio . . . You should be an actor, not some . . . peon.'

Glenn laughed and I sipped at my coffee. 'Thanks . . . I think,' he said.

I lifted one shoulder and kept eating.

'So, you got gas money?' Glenn asked.

I paused with a forkful of food halfway to my mouth. Gas money? How much did gas actually cost? And how much would he need to get to L.A.?

It doesn't matter, a little voice in my mind said. *You have to get a ride with this guy or you're stranded.*

'Of course,' I replied, shoving the food into my dry mouth.

'Great,' Glenn said with a grin. My heart replied with a thump. His smile was even more stunning than his eyes. 'Then it looks like I have a travelling partner. We should be in L.A. by tonight.'

It was the most beautiful sentence I had ever heard.

Chapter 27

'I thought you might want to take breakfast in your room this morning, miss,' Asha said, carrying a tray into Carina's bedroom.

I could have kissed her. It was ten o'clock in the morning, Vineland time, and I was starving. I'd been up for hours, but I had no idea where the kitchen was and I didn't want to get caught snooping around the palace in the middle of the night. If someone caught me, they'd probably be a little bit suspicious when they realised that Princess Carina didn't know her way around her own house.

'Thank you so much, Asha,' I said as she arranged plates and glasses on the small table by the window. She lifted one of those silver domes you always see in movies to reveal waffles and fresh fruit and cream. I dug in right away.

'Your mother asked me to tell you that she and the king would see you later today,' Asha said, moving towards the bed. 'She's going straight from the airport to the hospital.'

I paused with a wad of waffle in my cheek, my heart dropping. 'Um . . . does she know?'

'Know what, miss?' Asha asked as she smoothed the sheets and fluffed the pillows.

'About what happened back . . . back in the States?' I asked.

Asha stood up straight and looked at the floor. 'May I be perfectly honest, miss?' she asked. She was acting like she was afraid to look at me.

'Uh-huh,' I said, trying to swallow.

'Everyone knows about it, miss,' she said. 'It's been in all the papers. Your father was going to stay in Sweden for a few extra days, but he's cut his trip short to come back and . . . speak with you.'

You mean kill me, I thought. Oh God. Not only was I going to have to meet Carina's parents but they were going to be screaming at me the whole time. If they didn't recognise me and send me to the dungeon first. Which they would. Recognise me, I mean. I was sure they didn't really *have* a dungeon around here. Right?

'I just thought you'd like a warning,' Asha said, risking a glance in my direction.

'Thank you. I really appreciate it.'

'You're welcome, miss,' Asha said with a small smile. She finished making the bed as I attempted to eat. Unfortunately, my appetite had been severely damaged. The moment Asha excused herself from the room, I grabbed the phone.

'Call Ingrid,' I told the mystery guy on the line.

'Hello?' Ingrid said, picking up on the first ring.

'When the hell is Carina getting back here?' I blurted.

'Well, good morning to you, too,' she said.

'Ingrid, I'm serious. The king is coming home to ream her out for what she did with Markus.'

'What *you* did with Markus, you mean,' she replied.

I squeezed my eyes shut. 'Of course, but who cares? When he gets here, he's going to take one look at me and realise I'm not his daughter. If Carina doesn't get back here soon, I'm screwed.'

'Actually, there's a chance he won't realise a thing,' Ingrid said.

'What!? He's her father!'

'Yeah, but it's not like Carina has seen him for more than five minutes at a time in the last two years. You could be six inches taller and he'd probably just think he'd missed a growth spurt.'

I felt my stomach turn. 'Seriously?' I asked. 'That can't be true.'

'Well, I guess we're about to find out.'

A few hours later I couldn't take being locked up in Carina's room any more, waiting for her father to walk in and hand me my head. I decided to get out of there and try to find my way around. I kept thinking about the library I'd seen in one of Carina's books and figured that might be a good place to waste some time. Maybe I could find a book on Vinelandish law and see if they had any specific policies on royal imposters or punishments for impersonating a princess.

The castle was deathly silent, and for a while I didn't see another living soul. Most of the rooms in Carina's wing were bedrooms that looked like they hadn't been used in years. They were all decorated in the same classic style as Carina's room, and they were all perfectly clean. I couldn't imagine growing up in a place where there wasn't one speck of dust or one toy flung on the floor.

I made my way downstairs, tiptoeing whenever I heard voices or any kind of movement. I walked towards the back of the castle, dimly recalling that the library was in the south wing. But every door I opened revealed another parlour or seemingly pointless room filled with artwork and little couches. Finally I came to a pair of huge, intimidating wooden doors. I hesitated in front of them, worried that I might open them and find a crowd of Vinelandish dignitaries writing laws or something.

You're the princess, I told myself. *You can go wherever you want.*

I took a deep breath and yanked open the doors. There was a long table stretching down the centre of a grand room and at least ten workers were setting it with white china and sparkling silver. They all froze the moment they saw me.

'Oh . . . sorry,' I said automatically.

A man in a tuxedo stepped away from the others and bowed. 'Can I help you, Miss Carina?' he asked.

Okay, just chill out, I told my beating heart. *You're supposed to be in charge here.*

'Actually, I was looking for the library,' I said, biting my lip. 'I know it sounds weird, but I forgot where it is.'

The man smiled. 'That doesn't sound weird at all, miss,' he said, prompting the other servants to smirk and look away. I guess Carina wasn't big on the library. 'Just follow me.'

I let out a sigh of relief and did as I was told, following the man through hallways and a few more of those pointless rooms until he opened the doors to the library. My mouth dropped open when I saw the shelves upon shelves of colourfully bound books. The servant bowed as I walked past him into the room. I stepped right into the centre and turned around and around, my head tilted back to take it all in.

'It's amazing,' I said.

'Enjoy yourself, miss.' Again I did as I was told. I ran up the steps, checking out the different sections. There was a whole wall dedicated to world history and another dedicated just to the history of Vineland. I found the fiction section, which had first editions of everyone from Hemingway to Hawthorne to Alice Walker and Sandra Cisneros. Forget about spending hours in here. I could have spent days!

I walked up and down the rows and rows of books, pulling a few out here and there and flipping through the pages. When I came around the corner into a section marked Art and Architecture, I froze in my tracks. Markus was standing five feet away from me, his nose buried in a book. I would have thought I was seeing things if he hadn't looked up and immediately dropped the huge book on the floor, causing what was probably the loudest noise the room had ever suffered.

'Carina!' he said loudly.

'Markus,' I replied in a whisper.

'What are you doing here?' we both said at the same time. Then we laughed.

'My father thought I should come back and apologise to

your father in person,' Markus said, picking up his book and replacing it on the shelf. 'He's out riding on the grounds somewhere with Duke Charles, but I thought I would wait in here. This is my favourite room in the palace.'

'Oh,' I said. 'Mine too.' My head was so filled with other things I wanted to say, I couldn't sort through them. I had thought I would never see Markus again. And now here he was, walking towards me. 'I . . . do you know when my father's coming back?'

'Soon,' Markus replied. He reached out and took my hand, lacing my fingers through his, all the while looking me right in the eye. 'Carina, I'm so sorry. If I had thought that anyone would see us—'

'I know,' I said. 'And it's not your fault. I was there, too, remember?'

'Yeah, but we know how our parents think,' he said. 'I'm supposed to be the man. I'm supposed to be responsible.'

'Well, that's just dumb,' I said.

Markus laughed, then released my hand and leaned back against one of the hulking shelves. My hand felt insanely cold the moment he let go of me.

'I just wish we'd *seen* that photographer,' he told me, shaking his head. 'I would have ripped the film right out of his camera.'

'Who was it anyway?' I asked.

'Some paparazzi guy who was hanging around outside hoping to get some pictures of you,' he said. 'He's probably rolling in money by now.'

'What a way to make a living,' I said, leaning back next to him.

Markus took a deep breath, then turned to look at my profile. 'Listen, if our parents ever let us see each other again . . . do you think you'd like to . . . go out for dinner or something sometime?'

My heart felt like it was shrivelling up right under my skin. He sounded so uncertain and so hopeful. And all I wanted to do was say yes. But I couldn't. He wasn't asking me, he was asking Carina. And Carina didn't want to have anything to do with Markus.

What was wrong with her? Why couldn't she see how perfect he was?

I took a deep breath and turned to face him. The expectant look in his eyes made me want to run from the room. 'Markus, I—'

Suddenly the doors to the library burst open with what was now the loudest noise this room had ever suffered. Markus and I jumped apart. Although we couldn't see the doors from where we were standing, I had a feeling I knew who was there.

'Carina!' a voice bellowed. 'Carina! I know you're in here somewhere! Get down here this instant!'

Oh God, just let me disappear! I thought desperately.

'Let me explain,' Markus said squeezing my hand. Then he walked out from behind the shelves.

'Your Majesty,' he said confidently.

'Markus,' I heard the king say. 'Where's my daughter?'

Shaking from my fingers all the way down to my toes, I stepped out next to Markus, my head down. There was no way I could let this man see my face. What was he going to do when he realised I wasn't his daughter?

'Carina, I think the least you could do at this moment is show me the respect of looking me in the eye,' Carina's father said, clearly trying to control his voice.

Here goes nothing.

I lifted my chin and waited for the next explosion. The king stood on the floor below us – we were one set of stairs up from the main floor of the library. He was wearing a three-piece suit and his blond hair was slicked back from his face. He was a tall man, a bit on the hefty side but definitely strong. His face was bright red with anger.

But there was no spark of surprise. No spark of recognition.

'How could the two of you be so irresponsible?' he said, his voice level.

Oh my God. Ingrid was right. Carina's father didn't even know her well enough to know that I wasn't her!

'Sir, let me explain—'

'I'd rather hear from my daughter first,' the king said, raising a hand to stop Markus. 'Come down here, Carina.'

Somehow I made it down the steps on weakened legs. Maybe when I got a little closer to him. Maybe when he looked into my eyes. Maybe then he would realise. Suddenly I found myself hoping that he would. If he didn't see that I wasn't his daughter . . . The thought was just too sad.

I took a few steps towards him and looked into his face. My heart was pounding so loudly I was surprised neither he nor Marcus seemed to hear it.

'How many times have I told you that the image you project reflects on the rest of your family?' he said. 'On the rest of your country. Do you even realise the gravity of what you've done?'

'All I did was—' I stopped because my voice had cracked. I cleared my throat and started again. 'All I did was go out with a guy that you've been trying to set me up with since birth,' I said, my Vineland accent faltering a bit.

'Don't take that tone with me,' he replied, shaking. 'You both know that a princess is not supposed to run around with a young man unsupervised. I don't care who the young man is.' He glanced at Markus, and Markus walked down the steps to stand next to me.

'Sir, I can assure you that nothing improper happened,' he said. 'Carina conducted herself as a lady the entire time and—'

'And Markus was a perfect gentleman,' I added.

'Don't you realise it doesn't matter?' the king said, pacing away from us. 'It doesn't matter what you *say*. All that matters is what people want to *believe*. Like it or not, our world is all about appearances, Carina. I can't believe that my daughter would do something like this.'

At that moment the tears that had been welling up in my eyes – tears of frustration, of fear, of confusion, of sorrow for Carina – spilled over. Something inside me snapped. I was exhausted. I'd been through too much over the last few days. And everything came bubbling to the surface at once.

'I can't listen to this any more!' I shouted, causing the king to whirl around at me.

'Carina!' he bellowed.

'I don't want to hear about the respect I owe you or

how I'm supposed to act!' I yelled through my tears. 'I don't owe you anything! You don't even know me! You don't even know your own daughter!'

'Carina, calm down,' Markus said, reaching out to me.

I slapped his hand away and his whole face fell. At that moment I wanted to tell them. I wanted to tell them both and explain everything and let the fallout come. But I couldn't. I was sure if I tried, it wouldn't make any sense anyway.

And besides, it wasn't my place. I had to let Carina figure out what she wanted to do about her own relationships. These people had nothing to do with me. Not the king and not Markus.

So instead I simply turned and ran out of the library, leaving them both stunned and silent behind me, just hoping I could find my way back to Carina's rooms.

And hoping neither one of them would follow.

Chapter 28

'Wait a minute, wait a minute,' Glenn said as he pulled the car to a stop in front of a gas pump. 'Are you actually telling me that you think Julia Roberts is the greatest American actress of our time?'

'Yes,' I said, raising my eyebrows. 'You don't?'

'Please! What about Julianne Moore . . . Holly Hunter . . . Meryl Streep . . .'

He climbed out of the car, still talking, and I did the same. We'd been discussing movies for the past two hours on the road and Glenn had some very strong opinions on the subject, all of which I disagreed with. He thought that Steven Spielberg was overrated, that all teen genre movies made in the last ten years should be destroyed, and that Gwyneth Paltrow wasn't even pretty.

Maybe I *had* accepted a ride with an insane person. Besides, people were always saying *I* looked like Gwyneth, so if *she* wasn't pretty . . .

'So you don't think she should have won an Oscar for *Erin Brockovich*?' I asked him, slamming the car door behind me.

My leg muscles were all tight and my back ached in a million places. I stretched my arms over my head and yawned, then recovered myself. I couldn't do that type of thing in public.

Yes, you can, a little voice in my head reminded me.

I smiled and stretched again. I'd been having a lot of these little internal realisations all day. Like when I realised I didn't have to sit with my legs crossed at the ankle. Or when I passed Glenn a map from the glove compartment, then slammed the little door on my finger and let out a curse. For a moment I had cringed, waiting for Fröken Killroy's screech in my ear, and then I had realised she was thousands of miles away. So I cursed again. It felt really good.

'Are you kidding me? Joan Allen was robbed!' Glenn said, shoving the gas pump into his car. 'She was unbelievable in *The Contender*.'

I furrowed my brow in an exaggerated way. 'Do you have a thing for older women?' I asked.

Glenn blushed. 'No. Just real actresses.'

I smiled and leaned back against the car, tipping my face towards the sun. I couldn't remember the last time I'd had a real conversation with a guy. Actually, it had probably never happened. All Markus ever wanted to talk about was school and his polo and my goodwill tours. He didn't make me laugh like Glenn had all morning. And if I'd cursed in front of him, he'd probably have been appalled.

But then, Glenn did remind me of Markus in other ways. Good ways. Like when we'd stopped at this little tourist information place to use the bathroom, he'd opened the door for me. Markus always did that. Well, most people in Vineland did that for me. But everywhere I'd gone with Ribbit the night before, he'd cut ahead of me and gone in first – the dressing room after his act, the club after the dressing room, the bus after the club. Plus Glenn kept asking me if I was hot or cold or if I wanted the stereo on or off. He wanted to make sure I was comfortable, which was another Markus-type thing to do. And when I talked, Glenn really listened. Markus always really listened. Even when I was just talking about Heinrich the Lisper or Ingrid's latest whatever.

I sighed and looked down at my scuffed sandals, my heart feeling heavy. I guess Ribbit had just turned out to be a frog and today I'd met a prince. One who had made me think about the prince I had waiting back home all along.

Wait a minute. Was I *missing* Markus?

'You okay?' Glenn asked as he put the pump thing back on its hook.

'Um . . . yeah,' I said, shaking my head to try to clear the very un-me thoughts. Since when did I want to spend any time around Markus?

'Good,' Glenn said. 'Cuz I need your gas money.'

'Oh! Right!' I grabbed my bag out of the car and sifted through it for what was left of my American dollars – a ten and a five. I pulled out the crumpled bills and handed them to Glenn.

'Perfect,' he said. 'This'll just cover it.'

I swallowed hard as he walked off into the gas station with the last of my money. That was all I could pay for?

One gas stop? What was I supposed to do for the rest of the day?

I opened the car door and sat down sideways on my seat, resting my head in my hands. *You'll be all right,* I told myself. *It's just one day. You've come this far.*

Glenn returned from the shop, carrying a bag of pretzels and two bottles of water.

'Thought you might want a snack,' he said, handing everything to me.

I smiled, relieved. I would just have to make these pretzels last a few hours. Glenn really was a gentleman. He was totally changing my mind about normal people. Apparently they weren't *all* rude.

'So . . . I bet you think Tom Cruise is a good actor, too,' Glenn said with a challenging smile as he climbed back into the car.

I slammed my door and stared him down. 'You are a traitor to your own society.'

Glenn laughed, revved the engine, and raced back out onto the road.

That evening I sat down at a table in a restaurant called International House of Pancakes across from Glenn. Just like the restaurant we'd been in that morning, the smells in this place were making my stomach grumble, but this time it was even worse. Because this time I had no money to pay for food.

'I can't believe you've never been to an IHOP,' Glenn said, sliding an immense menu over to me. 'Their buttermilk pancakes are like heroin.'

My stomach dropped. 'Do you *do* heroin?' I whispered, stunned.

Glenn laughed. 'No. It's just an expression. So what are you going to have?'

'Nothing,' I said nonchalantly, closing the menu to block out the scrumptious-looking photos of crepes and waffles and fruit. 'I can't eat breakfast for dinner. It's too weird.'

'They have dinner food,' Glenn said, opening my menu again to a page full of steaks and pasta and salad.

'I'm not hungry.' I slapped the menu closed again.

'You have to be kidding,' Glenn said. 'You haven't eaten anything besides pretzels since this morning.'

'I'm fine,' I said firmly, wanting to drop the subject.

A waitress came over and put two glasses of ice water on the table. 'What'll you kids have?' she asked.

'I'll take the hearty breakfast combo and a Coke,' Glenn said.

'And you?' the woman asked me, taking Glenn's menu.

I'll have everything, I thought. *Pancakes and sausage and bacon and fruit cup and . . .*

'Nothing for me,' I replied.

As she walked away, a cell phone started to ring. Glenn dug in his backpack and pulled out a tiny black phone. He took one look at the number on the caller ID and his whole face hardened. He turned the phone off without answering it.

'Who was that?' I asked.

'My sister,' he replied, dropping the phone back into his backpack. He averted his gaze and took a sip of his water, then started crunching on some ice.

'You guys don't get along?' I asked, sipping at my own

water. I could feel it run down my throat and into my empty stomach.

'It's a long story,' Glenn said, looking across the restaurant. 'Short version is, my dad just died and he really wanted to see my sister, you know, before . . .' He took a deep breath and pushed his glass back and forth on the table between his hands, leaving a little trail of water. 'Anyway, we buried him a couple of weeks ago and she never even came to the funeral.'

'Oh,' I said, suddenly forgetting all about my empty stomach. 'I'm so sorry about your dad.' I had a strange impulse to give him a hug. And I never felt like hugging anyone. 'Were he and your sister . . . fighting?'

'Not any more,' Glenn said, glancing at me for a split second before looking away again. 'They hadn't talked in a long time. My parents had a messy divorce and Gina – that's my sister – she blamed my dad. I just think . . . you only get one family. I just know she's gonna regret that she didn't forgive him before he . . .'

Glenn trailed off and I felt a lump form in my throat. Back in Vineland my mother was sitting with my grandmother, basically watching her get weaker and weaker. And she was probably hating me for not going to see her, just like Glenn was hating his sister right now.

You only get one family . . .

Somehow I couldn't remember why I had refused to go see my grandmother. Oh yeah, because I thought I had better things to do.

'Anyway, Gina lives in L.A. and I'll see her when I get there. I'm just not ready to talk to her yet,' Glenn said. He

211

took a deep breath, then let out a long, loud sigh. 'Let's talk about something else.'

'Definitely,' I replied, pressing my sweaty palms into the vinyl couch.

'How about you tell me how it's possible you're not hungry right now?' Glenn said. 'I could eat a horse.'

My face burned and I took another sip of my water. The last thing I wanted to do was admit that I was penniless. What if he got mad and just left me here because I couldn't pay for more gas?

But what if you stop *for more gas and he asks you for money and you don't have it?* a little voice in my head asked.

I took a deep breath and looked at Glenn. He'd just poured his heart out to me. And he didn't seem like the type of person who would leave a girl stranded in the middle of nowhere. He'd already saved me from that fate once today.

'Okay, here's the thing,' I said. I closed my eyes and said it in a rush. 'I don't have any more money.'

'What?' Glenn said.

I opened my eyes, feeling queasy. 'That gas money I gave you was the last of it.'

'Why didn't you say something?' Glenn asked.

'I was afraid that you—'

'Did you think I wouldn't give you a ride?' Glenn leaned his elbows on the table. 'I only asked for gas money because I'm kind of short on cash lately. But if you're in some kind of trouble—'

'You have no idea,' I replied, surprised by the tears that sprang to my eyes.

The waitress placed Glenn's plate full of food on the table and I grabbed a napkin, pressing it under my eyes to keep myself from crying.

'Excuse me?' Glenn said before the waitress could get away. 'She changed her mind. She'd like to order.'

The waitress smiled at me sympathetically. 'What'll you have?'

'Glenn, I can't take your money,' I said, almost not believing the words that were coming out of my mouth. 'You've done more than enough already.'

'Carina, order something,' Glenn said. 'Or I *will* leave you here.'

I laughed through my almost tears and looked up at the waitress. 'I'll just have some grilled chicken and a salad, please,' I said.

'You got it,' the woman said, winking at me.

Glenn eyed me curiously across the table. 'So, you gonna tell me?' he asked.

'It's a long story,' I said, repeating his words back to him. 'Short version is, I fell asleep on a rock band's tour bus last night and ended up in the middle of the desert with no cash.'

'Ah, the life of a groupie,' Glenn said with a grin.

'But I can pay you back,' I told him. 'I'll send you the money, I swear.'

Glenn scoffed and leaned back in his seat. 'Please. I'm gonna be the next Heath Ledger or Brad Pitt, right? I don't need your money.'

I smiled and looked down at his untouched plate. 'Are you going to eat that?'

'I'll wait for yours to get here,' he said, lifting one shoulder.

'You really are a gentleman,' I said.

'Well, my dad raised me right,' Glenn said, his face growing serious.

'He really did,' I replied. 'He sounds like he must have been a good man.'

'Thanks,' Glenn said. 'He was.'

We both sat back and fell into a comfortable, thoughtful silence. When I got back home, the first thing I was going to do was go to see my grandmother. Then I was going to find a way to send Glenn the money I owed him. For the first time in my life, someone was doing something for me because they wanted to, not because they had to. And it felt . . . nice.

I had a feeling I was never going to forget this moment.

Chapter 29

That evening Glenn and I got lost in Los Angeles for almost an hour as I tried to find Julia's apartment building. Every time I'd been there, B.B. had driven us and I definitely hadn't been paying attention. Finally I saw a street name I recognised.

'Turn here!' I said, grabbing Glenn's arm.

'How good of a friend is this person you're staying with?' he asked, cutting the wheel. 'It's like you don't even know where she lives.'

'Another long story,' I said quietly. 'But this is the right street. It's that building up there. The one with the red door.'

Glenn pulled the car up next to the kerb and put it into park. I looked at him, temporarily at a loss for words. He had no idea what he'd really done for me that day. He was basically a hero. If we'd been back in Vineland, they'd have thrown a parade for him – the guy who rescued the princess from the desert.

'So . . .' Glenn said.

'So . . .' I repeated, looking down at my hands. 'Glenn, thank you so much for . . . for everything.'

'Not a problem,' Glenn said. 'It was kind of nice to have some company.'

'Would you give me your address? I'd like to send you back the money for dinner and everything.'

'It's okay. Really,' Glenn said.

'Fine, then just give me your address so I can send you a postcard or something someday,' I said, obviously lying.

Glenn shook his head but backed down. 'Okay, fine.' He reached past me and popped open the glove compartment, then dug through all the stuff inside and came out with a pen and a piece of paper with writing all over it. Glenn scratched his name and address out on the corner, then ripped it off and handed it to me.

'Thanks,' I said. As I pulled out my wallet to tuck his address away, a couple of my Vinelandish bills flew out and landed on the console between me and Glenn. My stomach lurched as Glenn picked them up.

'What're these?' Glenn asked.

'Oh . . . nothing,' I replied, grabbing for them.

He pulled his hands away and turned the bills over. 'The Republic of Vineland?' he read, glancing at me. 'Where'd you get these?'

'Um . . . Vineland?' I replied, taking the money back and stuffing it in my wallet.

'When did you go to Vineland?' he asked. 'And why do you have all that money and no American money?'

I slumped back in my seat and looked at the ceiling. I was so close to getting away without having to explain.

'It's another long story,' I said. 'I'm kind of . . . from there.'

'Come on,' Glenn said, his blue eyes dancing. 'You don't have an accent.'

'Yes, I do,' I replied in my regular voice. It was such a relief to talk like myself again. 'This is what I really sound like.'

Glenn's eyes widened. 'Wow. You really *do* have a long story,' he said.

'I do,' I replied. 'And I'd love to tell you all about it, but I really have to go.' I popped open the door and Glenn grabbed my hand.

'Wait a minute,' he said. 'Promise me something.'

'What?' I asked, looking down at his hand over mine.

'You have to write to me and tell me the whole story,' Glenn said.

'Glenn—'

'Hey, I drove you from Arizona all the way to L.A.,' he said. 'The least you could do is tell me who you are.'

I smiled slowly, looking into those amazing eyes. 'Okay,' I said. 'You have a deal.' Then I squeezed his hand and stepped out of the car. Glenn waited until I was safely inside the building before pulling away. Ever the gentleman.

I took a deep breath and looked up the stairwell. I'd just finished one ridiculously hard part of my journey, but this could be even worse. How was I going to get into Julia's apartment to get her passport? What if her mother was home?

But it wasn't like I had a choice. I had no other way of getting out of the country. I just had to hope that Julia's mom was working like she'd been all week.I started up the steps, thinking of all the movies I'd seen where people had broken into houses with credit cards. Unfortunately, I didn't have any. Another downside of the whole never-having-to-pay-for-anything thing. Maybe Julia and her mother hid a key near the door somewhere like in *Ferris Bueller's Day Off.* That would be perfect. Of course, I could also probably get someone in the building to open the door for me. After all, I *was* Julia. I could just say I'd locked myself out.

When I got to Julia's apartment, I tried the doorknob and it was, of course, locked. I was about to check under the welcome mat when the door flew open and Julia's mother was standing there, her brown, unwashed hair up in a ponytail, her eyes wide with hope, holding a crumpled tissue in her hand.

I stood up straight, my heart in my throat. She just stared at me for a moment, looking utterly confused.

'Where's my daughter?' she asked me. 'You look just like—'

'I can explain,' I said.

She stepped aside, watching me with this sort of stunned expression as I walked by her. I made my way to the kitchen and sat down. The table was covered with notes that had names and phone numbers on them. One of them read *Vineland Embassy* and another was a number for the FBI. I swallowed back a lump that was forming in my throat. Julia's mother had really been worried. Suddenly Julia's cat hopped into my lap and I let her curl up there, purring. When Julia's mother came into the room, she stood at the end of the table, staring at me.

'You might want to sit down,' I said.

'I think I'll stand,' she replied.

So I took a deep breath and told her the whole story. Everything. From the sushi restaurant to the training to the makeovers to getting stranded on the bus. When she heard that Julia was in Vineland, she decided sitting down would be a good idea. Then I explained that I'd come back there to get Julia's passport so that I could go home and Julia could return to L.A.

'I'm really sorry,' I said when I was finished. 'If I'd had any idea that it was going to cause this much trouble . . .' I trailed off when I realised I was about to say that I wouldn't have done it. But I knew that I would have. Two days ago all that had mattered to me was meeting Ribbit and escaping from being a princess for a while. I would have done anything for that chance. Now all I wanted to do was go home.

'So . . . you're a princess,' Julia's mother said.

'Yes,' I replied.

'And my daughter is impersonating you in Vineland right now.'

'Yes.'

Julia's mother stood up, scraping back her chair, and marched into her bedroom. I sat at the table, scared to move, as I listened to her banging around for a few minutes, slamming drawers and muttering to herself. When she reappeared a couple of minutes later, she had on a pair of jeans and a sweater, and her dirty hair was all hidden under quite a beautiful red hat. She was carrying a suitcase.

'You'd better go get Julia's passport,' she said, grabbing up a huge wad of cash from the kitchen counter. 'We're going to Vineland.'

Chapter 30

I was sitting at Carina's desk with her furry white cat in my lap, surfing the web and waiting for someone to come and arrest me. It had been hours since my confrontation with the king, but I was sure he was going to figure out that Carina would never have talked to him like that. At least I didn't think she would have. Did anyone ever yell at a king? Well, anyway, he had to realise that I wasn't his daughter. He just had to. And when he did, I was going to be in serious trouble.

There was a sudden knock at the window and I practically jumped out of my skin. I spun around to find Ingrid standing at the glass doors that led out to the verandah. She waved at me hysterically and I jumped up to let her in, sending the cat flying. He let out an angry yowl and disappeared under the bed.

'Thank you!' Ingrid said, all out of breath as she ducked into the room. 'I paid off one guard to let me onto the grounds, but if I'd been out there much longer, someone would have definitely caught me.'

'How did you get up here?' I asked as Ingrid sat down on the bed.

'Climbed up the trellis,' she said. 'Do it all the time. It's easier for Carina to sneak *out*, but I sneak in when necessary.'

'They won't let you in the front door?'

'Not after hours. And not tonight,' Ingrid said, getting control of her breath.

'Why not tonight?' I asked.

'There's some kind of dignitary dinner going on here. People higher up than my parents. The king and queen are probably doing damage control for you and Markus.' She looked me up and down and her forehead furrowed. 'Why aren't you dressed?'

'I . . . I didn't know,' I said, standing up. 'Are you telling me I have to go to this thing?'

'Well, Carina's not back yet, so—'

'But won't the queen be there?' I asked desperately. I felt like I was going to explode from stress and fear and guilt. I couldn't take it any more. I half *wished* the Vineland police would get their butts in here and arrest me.

'You have a point,' Ingrid said. She pulled her phone out of her pocket and checked for messages. 'Where is she?'

'That's what I'd like to know,' I said.

There was a knock on the door and my heart dropped. 'Uh . . . who is it?' I called.

'It's Asha, miss. I came to help you get ready.'

I shot Ingrid a doomed look. 'Better just let her in,' she said.

'Come in!' I called out, sinking back into the chair.

Asha bustled through the door with an armful of gowns and laid them out carefully on the bed. A slim purple gown, a puffier pink thing, a blue dress that looked exactly like something Jennifer Garner would wear to an awards show. Ingrid stood up and we both watched Asha as she worked. A heavy dread settled in over the room and I knew Ingrid and I were both feeling it.

'What time will dinner be served, Asha?' Ingrid asked.

'Seven o'clock, Miss Ingrid,' she replied, smoothing out the last gown, a deep red strapless dress with one glittery asymmetrical stripe down the left side. 'Now, princess, which would you like to wear?'

None of them, I thought. *I just want my own jeans and my own sneakers and I want to go home.*

Ingrid nudged my shoulder and I sighed. 'I guess the red one,' I said, standing.

'Excellent choice,' Asha told me, lifting the dress and draping it over my arms. 'I'll go get your red pumps and your tiara. Will there be anything else?'

'How about an escape ladder,' I muttered.

Asha smiled. 'I'll see what I can do, miss,' she joked before hustling out of the room.

'I actually gave Carina one of those once, but they took it away,' Ingrid said.

I looked at her, the dress hanging limply from my arms. 'What are we going to do?'

Ingrid lifted her hands, palms up. 'Get you dressed and hope for a miracle.'

I stood in front of the mirror in Carina's room in the most beautiful dress I'd ever seen, wearing a tiara, with a set of real rubies draped around my neck. I should have been breathless with excitement. Instead I was breathless with fear.

'It's almost seven,' I said to Ingrid, who stood by the window frantically dialling her phone. She had put on one of Carina's other dresses just in case she needed to go downstairs and do . . . *something* to stop what was about to happen.

'I know this,' she said, holding the phone up to her ear. 'Ugh! It keeps saying she's out of the calling area, but we both have worldwide service! Even if she's still in L.A., I should be able to get her.'

'Don't say that! She can't still be in L.A.,' I said, my stomach doing back flips.

There was a quick knock on the door and then Asha peeked her head in. 'They're expecting you downstairs, miss.' Then she disappeared again.

'I'm not going,' I said to Ingrid. 'They can't make me go.'

'Actually, they can,' Ingrid said. 'The king once sent the guards up to drag Carina downstairs for a holiday brunch. Of course, Carina *was* being a brat that day. Something about hating the new chef.'

'Oh God. I'm really going to be sick,' I said, holding my hand over my stomach. Suddenly the tiara felt like it weighed a thousand pounds and was squeezing into my head. My temples started to throb and my vision swam. Ingrid walked over to me and clutched my arm, half holding me up.

'Okay, we are going to walk down there together and I will tell the queen . . . something,' Ingrid said. 'This whole thing was my idea. I'll . . . I'll tell her.'

I swallowed back the bile in my throat and looked at her. 'Really?' I asked. 'If you're lying to me again, I'll—'

'I swear I'm not lying,' Ingrid said, releasing my arm. 'Julia, I'm really sorry about everything. Really.'

I took a deep breath, calming my nerves. 'It's okay,' I said, raising my chin. 'This isn't entirely your fault.'

After all, I had agreed to take Carina's place. I had flirted with Markus and hurt Ingrid's feelings. I could have . . . I don't know . . . faked a seizure or something before the plane had taken off for Vineland. We were in this together now.

We both turned and looked at the open door as if it were the gateway to hell. Ingrid reached out and clasped my hand. I squeezed hers back.

'You ready?' I asked.

'Let's go,' Ingrid replied.

We walked out into the hallway, hand in hand, and managed to descend the long, winding staircase without tripping ourselves out of nervousness. When we reached the front hall, I saw the queen ushering a few guests through the doors on the far side of the room. I couldn't breathe to save my life.

'Here goes nothing,' Ingrid said.

The queen turned around and saw us from across the room. She tilted her head with a motherly look of disappointment, then smiled and shook her head. It was like she was upset about the whole Markus thing but at the same time not all that surprised.

She started across the room towards us, and for a moment I thought it was going to be a replay of the scene with the king – that she wasn't going to recognise me. But when she was about ten yards away, her face suddenly dropped. My grip on Ingrid's hand tightened and she clasped me back so hard I thought my fingers were going to break.

The queen's hand fluttered to her chest and she looked me right in the eye. Then she said the words I'd been expecting to hear since this whole charade started:

'Who *are* you?'

Chapter 31

The taxi pulled up to the front gate at the palace and stopped. I was so tense, I was tempted to tell the driver to just smash right through it. Ever since the moment I'd stepped off the plane in Vineland International, I had been bombarded with images of Julia and Markus – on the TVs at the airport, on the cover of every newspaper – with headlines like RENEGADE PRINCESS and FINGER-LICKIN' CARINA! I had tried to call Ingrid from my cell phone to find out what was going on, but my battery was completely dead. I had no idea what Julia and Markus had done, but if I knew my parents at all, she was either locked in my room still waiting to be screamed at, or the screaming had already happened and we were both in huge amounts of trouble.

Why had I ditched on my responsibilities? How had I ever thought Julia would be able to handle it? I'd been training to be me my entire life. Clearly a few crash courses hadn't been enough.

Joshua, one of the younger guards, approached the car and motioned for the driver to roll down the window.

'I'm sorry, but there's an event at the palace tonight and tours end at 5 p.m.—'

'Event? What event?' I blurted, leaning over the driver's shoulder.

'A state dinner, miss. It begins at seven.'

I jumped out of the back seat, my heart racing. I knew Josh all too well. Ingrid and I had paid him off so many times to get on and off the grounds, he had saved enough to buy a BMW last spring.

'Josh! You have to let us in!' I said, hanging on to the top of the car door.

'Miss, you'll want to get back into the vehicle,' he said, that blank, I'm-in-charge look on his face.

'Joshua! It's me! Princess Carina!' I said, looking up at him desperately. Whatever this state dinner was for, it was going to start in about five minutes from now. If I didn't get in there soon, Julia was going to be in major trouble. If she hadn't been found out already.

'Princess Carina is inside,' Joshua said with a smirk.

'Josh! You have to believe me! Look at me!' I said. The commotion had attracted the attention of the other gate guards. Marshall, Ricardo, and Morris all emerged from their little station houses and walked over to stand around Joshua.

'Is there a problem?' Morris asked, raising one eyebrow. He always thought that looked particularly threatening.

'Look, if you guys don't let me inside right now, I'm going to have every last one of you fired,' I said, causing them all to crack up laughing.

'Miss, if you don't get into the car right now, we're going to have you forcibly removed from the grounds,' Joshua said, reaching for my arm.

My eyes flashed. 'You touch me and I'll tell my father about all the times you let me and Ingrid off the grounds. I'll tell him about the hundreds of times you let Ingrid in. I'll even tell him that your car was paid for entirely out of my trust account.'

Joshua froze. He looked at the other guards, who were eyeing him warily. I stared right back at him with all the defiance I had in me and finally Josh narrowed his eyes. He bent towards me until he was just inches from my face.

'Princess Carina?'

'Are you going to let me into my own palace now?' I asked, tilting my head.

Josh took a stunned step back from the car and I slipped into my seat and slammed the door. He waved at Morris to open the gate, and finally the taxi was moving up the drive. When the palace came into view a few moments later, I almost burst into relieved tears.

'Wow. This place is unbelievable,' Julia's mother said.

'It's home,' I said.

I could barely contain myself as the taxi driver pulled around the front drive and stopped before our doormen. My whole body was taken over by butterflies. I had to get inside and see my parents. I had to get inside and save Julia. Ronald stepped forward and opened my door for me as if I was one of the dignitaries arrived for the dinner. I jumped out and tossed a bunch of bills through the window at the taxi driver, then bounced up and down on the balls of my feet while I waited for Ronald to help Julia's mom with her bag.

Soon we were both rushing up the front steps towards the palace. I had no idea what kind of scene might greet us behind those doors, but for once I wasn't worried about what was going to happen to me. I just wanted to bring Julia and her mother back together and put an end to this whole mess.

And I wouldn't mind seeing my own mother, either.

Chapter 32

'I asked you a question,' the queen said, taking a few steps closer to me. At that very moment Markus and his father walked in, decked out in tuxedos once again. Markus's face lit up when he saw me.

'Who are you and what are you doing in my daughter's clothes? In her crown?' the queen asked, her voice quavering.

'Your Highness, what are you talking about?' Markus asked, striding over to us. 'Are you quite well? This is your daughter.'

He touched my arm and I thought I was going to throw up right on the queen's very expensive-looking shoes.

'Actually . . .' I heard myself say.

And then the front doors to the hall burst open and Carina came flying into the room. Her hair was still brown and she was still wearing the same clothes she'd worn to the concert. She froze in her tracks when she saw us all standing there, taking in everyone's expressions. I knew she was sizing up the situation and trying to figure out what had been said. If she'd been five minutes earlier, she could have saved us all *a lot* of trouble.

'Hi . . . Mom,' Carina said, lifting a hand.

'Carina?' the queen said.

'Julia!?'

That was my mother. When I heard her voice, I thought I was finally losing it. But then she walked into the room and the moment she saw me, she dropped the suitcase she was carrying. I started crying before she even made it across the room.

'Julia! Are you all right?' she asked, hugging me so tightly I could hardly breathe.

'I'm fine, Mom,' I said. 'I'm so sorry.'

She pulled back and looked me over and I knew she wasn't mad. She was just as relieved to see me as I was to see her. The major freak-out would probably come later. When we were alone.

'Carina?' I heard Markus say. He stepped back from us and looked at me, then at the real Carina, his face contorting in confusion.

'Markus, I—'

'I'm Carina,' the princess said, walking a bit farther into the room. 'That's Julia Johnson. From L.A.'

Markus's eyes filled with pain, and I thought my heart was going to shrivel up and die right then and there. Even with my mother's arms around me and even with everything falling back into place, I had never felt so awful in my life.

'I didn't mean to—'

Markus turned on his heel and swept out of the room, past his father, who was calling his name, and past Carina, who tried to grab his arm. I had a fleeting thought of going after him and then the king strode into the room.

'What is going on out here? We have guests in the dining hall and the entire royal family is loitering in the front hall!' he bellowed.

'Reginald, we seem to have a bit of a problem,' the queen said, walking over to him and placing her hand on his arm. She looked from Carina to me and the king followed her gaze. His jaw opened slightly, then snapped shut.

'What . . . what is the meaning of this?' he asked.

'It's all my fault, Your Highness,' Ingrid spoke up suddenly. She rushed forward to stand in front of the king and queen and gave a quick curtsy.

'Ingrid, no,' Carina said, stepping forward and standing next to her friend. 'You're not taking the blame for this. It was my fault.'

I could tell Carina was shaking as she faced her parents, but she did her best to hide it. She lifted her chin and faced the music like . . . like a true princess.

'Mom . . . Dad . . . I'd like you to meet Julia Johnson,' Carina said, looking at me. 'I paid her to impersonate me on my last night in the States so that I could go to a rock concert.'

The queen's face fell in shock while the king quickly turned from red to a seriously disturbing shade of purple. Carina stepped back from him, anticipating a meltdown.

'Are you trying to tell me that this . . . this . . . *person* has been living in our home for the past two days *pretending* to be you!?' the king shouted, looking at me with so much disgust I wanted to slap him, king or no king.

'Yeah!' I shouted, moving away from my mother and towards the royal family, my skirts sweeping behind me. 'And you couldn't even tell the difference!' I said right to his face.

Carina looked at me, her mouth open and her eyes welling up with tears.

'How *dare* you speak to me that way!' the king shouted.

'Wait a minute, you really didn't notice she wasn't me?' Carina asked, a tear spilling over. She moved away from her parents, looking at them like they were aliens. 'Did you, Mom? Did you know?'

'Carina, of course I knew,' the queen said, walking up to Carina and wrapping her up in her arms.

'But Dad didn't,' Carina said, looking at her father, who finally seemed to realise what he'd done. He averted his gaze from his daughter and wife, clearly ashamed.

'Carina—'

'I know, go to my room, right?' Carina said, crying freely now. 'You just want me out of your sight. Like always!'

She pulled away from her mother and ran right by me and up the stairs. Ingrid turned to follow, but the queen laid a hand on her shoulder.

'I think her father and I should go,' she said softly,

looking at her husband meaningfully. Then she turned to Markus's father, who I'd forgotten was even in the room. He stood, hovering by the front door, clearly wishing he could disappear.

'Maurice, would you please go in and make our apologies to our guests?' the queen asked. 'Everyone is welcome to stay to dinner, but I don't believe we will be joining them.'

'Of course, Your Majesty,' Markus's father said with a quick bow.

Then the queen extended a hand to me. 'I am Victoria, queen of the Republic of Vineland,' she said.

I took her hand and curtsied as Carina had taught me to do. 'Julia Johnson,' I replied. 'And may I present my mother, Sharon Johnson.'

My mother shook hands with the king and queen. 'I'm sorry we have to meet under such . . . distressing circumstances,' the queen said, smiling at my mother. 'You know what it's like to have a teenager in the house.'

'Absolutely,' my mother said. 'It's a pleasure to meet you.'

The queen continued to smile at my mother, and then her eyes travelled up and rested on the red hat my mom was wearing. There was a moment of awkward silence in which my mother looked at me like, 'What's up with this woman?' and then the queen spoke again.

'I'm sorry, Ms Johnson, I was just noticing your lovely hat. Wherever did you get it?'

My mother reached up to touch the soft felt and blushed. 'Oh . . . I made it,' she said.

'Really?' the queen asked, obviously impressed. 'It's beautiful. Anyway, would you and Julia like to stay for a few days while we sort this all out?'

'We'd love to,' my mother said, looking at me again. I grinned back at her.

'Miss Goedecker,' the king said, turning to Ingrid, 'would you make sure our guests get settled in the east wing? We're going to go talk to our daughter.'

'Yes, Your Majesty,' Ingrid said with another curtsy.

Then Carina's parents started up the steps, arm in arm, talking in hushed voices. I looked at my mother, who was still blushing. But then she seemed to remember why, exactly, we were in a castle in a foreign country and her mouth settled into a straight line. I swallowed hard.

'So . . . ,' I said. 'You wanna kill me now or later?'

Chapter 33

I was face down on my bed, crying my exhausted eyes out, when I heard my parents approaching along the hall. The last thing I wanted was for them to find me having what they would call 'one of my tantrums'. Maybe they'd witnessed my breakdown in the front hall, but now I had to pull myself together. I was tired of being a big baby in their eyes.

I sat up, wiped my face with my hands, and pulled myself to the edge of the bed, swinging my legs over the side. The moment my bedroom door opened, I stood up to face them.

My mother walked in first. She swept right across the room and enveloped me in a hug. I grasped her back and held my breath to keep from crying again. When I saw my father, I turned away automatically. I couldn't even look at him.

'Carina, I don't know where to begin,' my mother said, sitting down on my bed and pulling me beside her. I could smell the lilac scent of her perfume, and it was bizarrely comforting. 'Are you all right? The thought of you alone in that city for the past couple of days . . .'

'I'm fine, Mom,' I said wearily. 'I took care of myself.'

I glanced at my father, who was just sort of hovering in front of us, clasping and unclasping his hands. He pressed his lips together and looked away when he caught my eye. I'd never seen my father look so uncertain of anything in his life.

'What happened over there?' my mother asked. 'What were you thinking, running away like that?'

Of course that was what they wanted to talk about. They wanted to know how I could have been so selfish and stupid and irresponsible. But my mother knew how I felt about the way my life was constantly planned out for me. This couldn't have come as that much of a shock to her. I was sure she was disappointed but not all that surprised. So why weren't we talking about my father and the fact that he didn't even know that Julia wasn't me?

I stared up at him, but he wouldn't even look at me. My heart hurt like my legs always did after a long ride or a marathon fencing lesson. Like it had been used too much and just couldn't deal any more. Like it wanted to collapse.

'Mom, I know you're mad and I'll explain everything,' I said. 'I'm just so tired . . . Can we talk about this in the morning?'

I just wanted them to go. I wanted my father gone so that I could stop feeling like this. Mom looked up at Dad with a question in her eyes, and for a moment I thought they were really going to give in. I was sure my father didn't want to wait around for me to remind him of what he'd done.

'I think we should talk about it now,' he said.

Suddenly a flash of anger took all the exhaustion right out of me. 'Fine!' I said, standing. 'If you want to talk, then let's talk about the fact that you didn't even realise that there was a stranger right under your nose! How do you think that makes me feel, Father?'

My eyes were brimming with tears again, but I wouldn't let them fall.

'That's exactly what I think we need to talk about,' my father said, finally looking me full in the face.

I was so taken aback that I sat right down again.

My father took a deep breath and let it out his nose, his nostrils flaring. 'Carina,' he said. 'I'm sorry. I . . . I cannot possibly imagine how much I've hurt you. I truly am sorry.'

I think my jaw hit the floor.

'Your mother always talks to me about how my travelling affects you. How my not being here affects you, but I've always told her . . . and you . . . that it's the way things are,' my father continued, starting to pace. He walked over to the door and then faced me directly. Another first. Eye contact during conversation was a big thing with my dad. 'I never saw my father. He never saw his. That's the life of a royal son or daughter. That's the way it always has been.'

'But that doesn't make it right,' I heard myself say.

My father turned to look at me and my mother. 'But that doesn't make it right,' he repeated.

I swallowed hard, unable to believe what I was hearing. Was my father really taking the blame for something? Was he actually admitting he was wrong?

'I was going to go back to Africa in a couple of days, but I think I'll cancel that,' my father said. 'The three of us have a lot of talking to do.'

Oh, great, I thought instantly. *A lot of talking.* But then I realised it actually *was* kind of great. I had never heard my father talk about ditching a commitment. Never. My parents exchanged a smile and I let one tiny tear spill over.

'Carina, I won't pretend what you've done wasn't wrong,' my mother said, taking my hand. 'And don't think that you aren't going to be severely punished,' she added, causing my stomach to turn. She squeezed my hand and looked up at my father. 'But maybe something good will come out of all this confusion.'

She stood up and gave me a hug, then ran her palm along my face, looking at me in that motherly way that always made me feel like I was five years old. But for the first time in a long time, it didn't make me flinch. Then I turned to my father, and suddenly he wrapped me up in his arms. My face was pressed against the medals he always wore on his breast for public events, but I didn't even care. My father was hugging me. Even Ingrid would never have believed this.

Maybe something good has already come out of this, I thought, smiling at my mother. And I could tell from the mistiness in her eyes that she was thinking the same thing.

Chapter 34

The conversation with my mother was shorter and a lot less shower-scene-from-*Psycho* than I'd thought it would be. She made me explain everything. She grounded me for six weeks, and then she told me we would talk more in the morning. The flight had made her extremely tired and she wanted to lie down. So Ingrid took her up to a room in the east wing and I went off to find Markus. (I figured my grounding wouldn't officially start until we were back on our native soil.)

The palace was huge and I could think of only one place to look. If Markus wasn't there, I knew I would never find him. I wasn't sure which way I would be better off – finding him or never seeing him again. But I had to at least try to apologise. I owed him that much.

After a few wrong turns I finally found my way to the library. I opened the doors as quietly as possible and stepped into the dark, silent room. The air was cold and a chill ran down my arms, bringing up goose bumps on my skin. I wrapped my arms around myself and tiptoed into the room.

'Markus?' I whispered.

There was a sudden movement a few feet away from me at one of the tables. My heart hit my throat and then a study light clicked on. Markus sat there, staring up at me, his face half shadowed, half bathed in the light.

'Who are you?' he asked harshly.

I walked over and pulled out the chair across from him. He followed me with his eyes as I tucked my skirt under me and sat down. I reached up, pulled the tiara from my hair, and placed it on the table between us. Markus looked at it blankly.

'My name is Julia Johnson,' I said. 'I'm sixteen years old . . . I live in L.A. and I go to a school called Rosewood Academy. I'm not a princess. I'm not even rich.'

His eyes narrowed at the last part, like money was the last thing on his mind – which I could imagine. I cleared my throat and sat up straight.

'I'm sorry I lied to you,' I said, my voice shaking. 'I'm sorry I pretended to be Carina. I—'

'Why did you do it?'

'She . . . she wanted to get away . . . see what it was like to not be a princess,' I said, raising my shoulders.

'And you? What did you get out of it?' he asked.

I really didn't want to answer that question. I watched him for a moment, hoping he'd relent, but his expression never changed. It was like he was a stone version of his formerly animated self.

'I . . . she . . . she paid me,' I said, looking down.

'You did this for money?' Markus said, standing up and almost knocking over his chair.

'We were about to get thrown out of our apartment!' I responded, standing up myself. 'Not everyone lives like you guys do, Markus. Not everyone gets to fly around the world and rent amazing cars and buy property the size of a small country!'

Markus shoved his hands in his pockets and stared at the floor. He clenched his jaw and I knew I'd got to him. When his gaze met mine again, there was a question in his eyes.

'Was anything you said that night—' He sighed and looked away. 'Was anything about that night true? Or did Carina just tell you to make an idiot out of me?'

'No!' I said, stepping closer to him. I was so relieved that he didn't move away. 'Carina didn't tell me to make an idiot out of you. I wasn't *trying* to make an idiot out of you.'

He glanced at me hopefully and I really wanted to just reach out and hug him, but I wasn't sure if he wanted me to. Standing there, so uncertain, with him only a foot away and still so untouchable, I felt very, very lonely.

'I just . . . I didn't expect to . . . like you so much,' I said, looking up into his eyes. My heart was pounding so hard I could barely hear myself think. 'I didn't expect to—'

'What?' Markus said, reaching out and taking my hand. 'You didn't expect to what?'

I looked down at our hands, completely overwhelmed by everything. By him, by this moment, by our surroundings, by the fact that no matter what I said, after tonight there was no way I could ever see him again. He was going to be some ministry head in Vineland and I was going to go back to being just another scholarship student at Rosewood.

So just go for it, I told myself. *You've got nothing else to lose.*

'I didn't expect to fall in love with you,' I said, tears filling my voice.

'I was so hoping you'd say that,' Markus said with a laugh.

I looked up at him and held my breath.

'I love you, too, Julia Johnson from L.A.,' he said with a heart-stopping grin. 'In one stupid night I fell in love with you.'

I laughed and he wrapped me up in his arms, lifting me off the floor. I was so totally relieved that I felt weak and limp and completely dizzy. When he replaced me on my own feet again, I held on to his arms for balance.

Then Markus touched my face with his fingertips, smiled a sweet little smile, and leaned in to kiss me. It was a kiss to end all kisses. And even though I knew it couldn't last, that this night would end and I'd have to leave him behind, I let myself go and decided to live the dream.

For the moment I was really a princess. And Markus was my prince.

Chapter 35

The following day I went, by myself, to the hospital to visit my grandmother. Her eyes lit up when she saw me, and she reached out her hand to hold mine. I sat next to her bed for an hour and told her all about my trip to California and about Ribbit and the bus and Glenn, my knight in a cotton T-shirt. My grandmother smiled and laughed through the whole story, then told me about a time when she was sixteen and she ran off to go skiing in the Alps with some guy named Gustav.

I thought I was actually going to fall out of my chair. Go, Grandmamma!

Finally the doctors told me she had to get some rest, so I promised I would be back tomorrow and headed home. The hospital was pretty much the only place I was allowed to visit for the next few weeks, so at least Grandmamma was a good excuse to get out of the house. Besides, I wanted to pump her for more stories of her crazy youth! Maybe she could give me some pointers.

Not that I was planning on running away again anytime soon. That morning I'd actually had breakfast with both my parents (and Julia and her mom). My father actually laughed over some of the stories Julia told about what it was like to be me. I think he's really starting to remember the way he felt when he was still a teenage prince. The whole family-esque feeling in the room was kind of cool.

On the way home from the hospital I chewed on my nails until there was practically nothing left to chew on. I had asked Markus to meet me at the palace at two o'clock, and I still hadn't figured out exactly what I was going to say to him. I knew I wanted to apologise for ditching him in the States and leaving him with Julia. And then there was going to be something along the lines of, 'Want to go out sometime after I'm off house arrest?' but I wasn't sure quite how to ask. Of course, the thing that was really tying my stomach in knots was the fact that I wasn't sure how he was going to react.

The night before, I had fought off exhaustion and spent hours on the phone with Ingrid, giving her the rundown of everything that had happened with Ribbit and Glenn. Then she'd spent another hour telling me everything that had happened with Julia and Markus. By the time that part of the conversation was over, I think I was even more red in the face than the time I'd gotten sunburned on the French Mediterranean.

According to Ingrid, it was perfectly obvious that Julia was now in love with Markus. My Markus! Hadn't I told her not to speak to him? How had she translated that into, 'Take my boyfriend out of the embassy on a secret rendezvous and fall in love with him?'

Okay, I know that when I talked to Julia, I told her that

I didn't want Markus. But after everything that had happened in L.A., I'd started realising exactly what I'd be giving up if I turned Markus down. He was handsome, and chivalrous, and smart, and athletic, and kind, and attentive. And apparently it wasn't that common to find all those qualities in one guy! Who knew?

Markus had been in love with me since we were toddlers and there was no way I was giving him up to Julia, no matter how good a friend she'd turned out to be. (After all, I don't think I would have got on a plane to a foreign country just to save her butt, or anyone else's for that matter.) Still, all was fair in love and war, right?

B.B. stopped the car in front of the palace and I didn't even wait for him to open the door for me. I ignored his expression of surprise and ran by him into the house. Markus was waiting for me in the south parlour. He stood up the moment I walked in.

'Carina,' he said with a smile. 'It's good to see you.'

'Markus,' I replied, walking up to him and kissing him on each cheek. 'I'm so sorry about what happened in America.'

'*I'm* sorry,' Markus replied. 'I'm the one who got your face in every tabloid in the world. Well . . . not *your* face, but—'

I sat down on the sofa and looked up at him through my lashes. 'I know. I feel like such an idiot for pulling off that stupid prank with Julia. I hope she didn't just drive you totally crazy.'

I watched his face for the minutest reaction at the sound of Julia's name, and my heart fell. He actually smiled this private sort of smile. Like he had some kind of . . . crush. Could Ingrid possibly be right?

'No. Not at all,' Markus said, leaning back on the sofa. 'Julia is . . .' He trailed off and stared off into space like a lovesick puppy dog.

'Great,' I said, slumping next to him. 'She's great.'

'Yeah, she is,' Markus said. 'And you know, I should have realised she wasn't you. I mean, you usually avoid me like I have onion breath when we go to those things, but Julia . . . she listened to me and laughed at my jokes and gave me advice.'

'I listen to you!' I protested feebly.

'Carina, come on,' Markus said. 'I usually bore you to tears.'

'That's not true!' I said indignantly, sitting up straight. He just looked at me, and I felt an embarrassed blush creep to my face. I stared down at my hands and fiddled with my sapphire ring.

'Okay, well, if I'm so awful, why do you still ask me to dance at all those functions?' I asked pitifully. 'Why do you even bother?'

'Because we're old friends,' Markus said, sitting up and taking my hand. 'And because you know if I didn't ask you to dance, we'd both hear it from our parents.'

I laughed, my heart heavy. 'You know,' I said, attempting a glance at him out of the corner of my eye, 'I was coming in here to ask you out on a date.'

'Really?' he blurted, raising his eyebrows.

'I know, crazy, huh?' I said.

'Carina, be honest,' Markus said, smiling. 'You don't

want a guy like me. You want a guy who'll sneak onto the grounds like Ingrid does and jet off with you to Paris on a moment's notice and . . . I don't know . . . a guy who wears a lot of leather and has tattoos and rides a black motorcycle or something.'

I laughed and blushed again. His assessment was pretty much dead-on.

'I'm too predictable for you,' he said lightly.

I took a deep breath and leaned back, slumping even farther into the couch. If my mother or Fröken Killroy walked in, I would be banished to my room with a book on my head. But I didn't care. It felt like a slumping moment.

'Well, I never would have predicted you were going to fall in love with my American double,' I said, looking up at him.

He turned crimson and sighed. 'Yeah. Me neither.'

Then we laughed again and he settled back. We sat there for a few moments, staring across the room at the portrait of my grandmother that hung above the fireplace. I wondered what her friend Gustav had looked like. And if he had a grandson.

'You know, I hear Gerald of Vistana just got back from partying in London for two weeks. His parents never even knew where he was. Maybe you should give him a call,' Markus said suddenly.

'I could never date a guy named Gerald,' I deadpanned, running a lock of my brown hair through my fingers. Gerald of Vistana was actually this total hottie with dark hair and brooding eyes who definitely deserved to have a better name.

'He has his own plane, you know,' Markus said.

'Interesting,' I replied. 'E-mail me his number.'

Markus smiled, leaned over, and kissed me on the cheek. There was no tingling skin, no heart palpitations, no loss of breath. Markus *was* a great guy, but he'd never been the guy for me. My prince was still out there somewhere. And I knew I'd have a lot of fun finding him.

Chapter 36

'Wait a minute, wait a minute,' I said, watching my mother in awe as she packed up her bag. 'You are going to be the official hat designer for the royal family?!'

'Yep,' my mother said with a grin. 'We are basically never going to have to worry about money again.'

'Mom! This is unbelievable!' I said, my heart bubbling over until my whole body felt fizzly. I ran over and hugged her, and she dropped the pair of jeans she was folding so she could hug me back. 'Do you have any idea how many hats you're going to sell when people back home find out about this?'

Her brow creased as she pulled away from me. 'I may have to hire a few people,' she said, biting her lip.

'You may have to start a whole company!' I added.

My mother smiled, piling a few more things into her suitcase. I wasn't sure if I had ever seen her look so relaxed and happy. And I definitely knew she'd never smiled for so long without stopping. Coming to Vineland might have been the best thing I'd ever done.

'Well, you can help me figure out a business plan with

all the free time you'll have when we get back home,' my mother said, snapping her suitcase closed.

My face fell. 'Don't I get any time off from my grounding for basically facilitating your meteoric rise to success?'

'Nice try, kid,' she said.

There was a knock at the door and she smacked my butt lightly, pushing me towards it.

'Ow!' I said jokingly as I scurried over to the door before she could whip me with the towel she'd used on her hair that morning. I was laughing as I pulled open the door.

'Markus!' I felt a full-body flush come on at the sight of him.

'I heard you were leaving today,' he said, glancing past me at my mom, who was eyeing us curiously. 'I thought we could go for a walk.'

'Oh! Yeah,' I said, my heart fluttering. I looked over my shoulder. 'Mom, this is Markus. Can I go for a walk with him? Just for a little while?'

Don't say I'm grounded, I begged silently. *I'll die if you say I'm grounded.*

'Hello, Markus,' my mother said, walking up next to me. 'I'm Sharon Johnson.'

'It's a pleasure to meet you, Ms Johnson,' Markus said, extending his hand.

My mother blushed. Seriously. I would have made a gagging sound if I hadn't been hoping she'd forget about my grounding.

'So, Mom?' I said when she drew her hand away. 'Can I?'

'Half an hour,' my mom told me sternly. 'You still

have to say goodbye to Carina and the king and queen.' She blinked and her forehead crinkled up. 'I can't believe I'm living in a world where I say things like that.'

'Get used to it,' I told her with a smile.

Markus and I were both silent for the first few minutes of our walk. It was a beautiful day out. The sun was shining and the air was warm and soft, much less heavy than the smoggy air in Los Angeles. I took in the immaculate lawns surrounding the castle, half trying to commit them to memory, half trying to calm my nerves. I wished Markus would talk first. There were so many things I wanted to say that I couldn't get them straight in my mind.

'What are you thinking?' Markus asked suddenly.

'I was just wondering what you were thinking,' I told him, trying to smile.

Markus laughed and led me towards a paved pathway that ran all the way out towards the thick woods behind the castle. We walked along the path until we came to a bubbling fountain surrounded by marble benches and shaded by trees. A breeze ruffled the branches overhead, letting the sun break through and cast leafy shadows on the water. It was really beautiful. I knew I would remember this place for ever.

'We should sit,' Markus said.

Something in his voice sent a shiver down my back. If I'd ever felt a sense of foreboding, that was it.

I perched on the bench next to Markus, afraid to move and afraid to get comfortable. I felt like I was waiting at the doctor's office for a shot. Something not good was definitely about to happen.

'Julia, I want you to know that I meant everything I said the other night in the library,' Markus said, leaning forward and resting his forearms on his thighs. He laced his fingers together and blew out a sigh.

'But . . . ?' I said, watching him carefully.

'But . . . there's no point in kidding ourselves,' Markus told me. 'This . . . what we have . . . it can't go anywhere.'

My stomach was tied in knots. Even though I knew he was right, hearing him say it was like hearing someone tell me I was never going to graduate or go to college. That I had no control over my future or getting the things I wanted.

'I'm really never going to see you again, am I?' I said, concentrating to keep my stomach in check.

Markus looked at me, and I knew the pain in his eyes was reflecting mine. 'I wish things were different, Julia, but you're going back to California, like you should. And I . . . I'm staying here to take over my father's post. Like I should.'

'But what about architecture school?' I blurted, suddenly forgetting about myself and my breaking heart. 'I thought you were going to talk to your father.'

Markus stood up and shoved his hands in his pockets. 'I was just daydreaming,' he said, looking off into the trees above my head. 'After everything that's happened . . . my father and I had a long talk and . . . I know what I have to do. I think I've always known.'

I was actually speechless, which was a really weird

feeling for me. How could he be so resigned to living a life he didn't want? How could he just give up like this?

'I know what you're thinking, but you've never met my father,' Markus said, flushing. 'He's kind of a master debater.'

'So he debated you out of your dreams?' I asked, a little too much sarcasm seeping into my voice.

'Not exactly. He reminded me of my duties,' Markus said, his jaw clenching. 'And I can still study architecture . . . as a hobby.'

'Is that gonna be enough?'

'It'll have to be,' Markus said. He tipped back his head and blew out a breath. I had this feeling that he wasn't telling me everything. That just like me, there were a million thoughts in his head and he was trying to sort through them all. 'You know what's funny?' he said finally. 'Everyone thinks that people like me are privileged. Like we can do whatever we want to do. But the truth is that people like you have a lot more freedom. You can make your own decisions in life.'

'So can you, Markus,' I said, standing up so that he had to look at me. 'You have to stand up to your father.'

Markus swallowed hard and looked me in the eye. 'I can't,' he said. 'This is the way things have to be. I have a duty to fulfil and you . . . you have your life to live.'

'Markus—'

'Julia, let's not talk about this any more. We only have . . .' He lifted his arm to check his watch. 'We only have fifteen minutes left. I don't want to spend it talking about my father.'

I sighed and reached up to hug him. When he held me, I felt like I just wanted to curl up in his arms and stay there. I forgot all about L.A. and school and my future. This was the only future I wanted to have – with Markus.

But the moment he let go, reality set in again. Markus's life was here in Vineland. He had to do what he felt he had to do. And I had to go home and get back to work on my own dreams. College, a career, a life of my own. I'd always promised myself I'd never let a guy make me forget about what I wanted. And even though Markus wasn't just some guy, I had to let him go.

'I'm really going to miss you,' I told him, looking up into his amazing eyes.

'I'm going to miss you, too,' Markus said, tucking my hair behind my ear. 'There's no one else in the world like you, Julia Johnson – no matter how many people you and Carina fooled.'

I smiled and wrapped my arms around his neck. 'Thanks for noticing,' I said.

Then Markus touched his lips to mine and we kissed goodbye. It was sweet, it was bitter, it was painful, it was heart-stopping. It was everything a goodbye kiss should be.

'I love you, Julia,' Markus said when we parted. 'I always will.'

Then he walked me back to my mother's room and we said goodbye. For ever.

Chapter 37

'So,' Julia said, sitting across from me on my bed with her legs pulled up under her. She was wearing a pair of comfy-looking jeans and a hooded tee. Her hair had been dyed back to its original colour, just like mine had. We were finally back to being ourselves.

'So,' I replied.

Ourselves, but slightly less articulate.

We looked at each other and laughed. For once in my life I was wishing for a speechwriter to tell me what to say. Julia was leaving to go back to L.A. in a few minutes and we were supposed to say goodbye. The problem was, there were about a hundred other things I wanted to tell her that seemed more important. And there wasn't enough time to say them all.

'Well . . . I have the rest of your money,' I said, reaching over to my bedside table and pulling an envelope out of the drawer. I dropped it on the bedspread between us.

'You don't have to pay me,' Julia said. 'It's not like I exactly did the job to your satisfaction. Thanks to me, you're no longer Princess Carina. You're the Finger-Lickin' Chick.'

I laughed, shrugging it off. 'That'll pass. Besides, being kidnapped to Vineland wasn't part of our deal. You more than earned it.'

Julia smiled and opened the envelope, fanning the cash inside with her thumb. 'Funny. It actually looks like I won't be needing this any more. Thanks to your mom and her monster hat order.'

'So blow it on a pair of really good shoes,' I said.

Julia blanched. 'Do they *have* five-thousand-dollar shoes?'

'Probably,' I replied. 'Even I don't know that.'

'Oh, they do.' Ingrid's voice cut into our conversation. 'I even tried on a pair once.'

I turned around to see her standing at the door to my balcony. 'How did you get in here?'

'Let's just say Josh will be purchasing some new rims for his Beemer,' Ingrid said, bouncing onto the bed. She sat down to my left, between Julia and me, as if she was going to officiate the conversation. I guess it was kind of appropriate, since she'd been our go-between all along. 'I couldn't miss saying goodbye to princess number two,' she said, smiling at Julia.

I took a deep breath and pulled my ankles a little closer to my body. 'So, Julia, you should know that I asked Markus out on a date.'

Julia honestly looked like I'd just told her I'd lost her scary little cat.

'He shot me down,' I told her.

'Really?' she said happily, then pressed her lips together, embarrassed.

'Yeah, he shot me down, too,' Ingrid said.

My heart hit my stomach. I hadn't just heard that. 'What?' I screeched. 'What are you talking about?'

'You asked him out, too?' Julia added.

'A girl's gotta do what a girl's gotta do,' Ingrid said, lifting one shoulder like we were talking about nothing more interesting than her new nail colour.

'Ingrid! You think Markus is more boring than toast points,' I exclaimed, totally confused.

'Carina, my friend,' she said, patting my knee. 'You are just really, *really* oblivious.'

I pulled back my head and blinked. 'I don't even know what to do with this information.'

'Well, don't worry about it. His heart belongs to Julia,' Ingrid said.

'Not exactly,' Julia told us with a sigh. 'We basically decided to call it off.'

Ingrid and I both looked at Julia, stunned. Normally I would have pumped her for more information – there's not much I love more than a good piece of juicy gossip. But something about the way she was avoiding looking at us made me stop myself. Yes. I was actually able to stop myself.

'Wow,' I said. 'Markus had a busy week.'

'I think we all did,' Julia said, raising her eyebrows.

'So, what're you going to do when you get back to L.A.?' Ingrid asked, settling back against my pillows and stretching out her legs so that her oversized feet were resting right between Julia and me.

'I don't know . . . Visit a Buddhist priest . . . go to a couple of movie premieres . . . maybe buy some cashmere,' Julia said, frowning comically. 'The usual.' She looked at me and grinned. 'Jealous?'

'Nah,' I said, leaning back on my hands. 'I'm going to try wearing these jeans out of my room. That should be enough excitement to last me *years*.'

Our laughter was cut short when Asha stepped into the open doorway. 'Miss Julia? The car is waiting to take you to the airport.'

Julia looked at me, and I got a sinking sensation all the way down to my stomach. In the last day I'd felt closer to her than I had after all those nights of coaching her back in the States. I actually didn't want her to leave.

'Well, you have my e-mail address,' Julia said, sliding off the bed.

I followed her lead and stood up across from her. 'And you have mine.'

'Carina, I wanted to say . . . I really am sorry for all the trouble I caused and for—'

'Stealing her boyfriend?' Ingrid supplied.

'Ingrid!' we both said at the same time.

'Well, I'm sorry for making your mother worry,' I said, rocking back on my heels. 'And for, you know . . .'

'Generally being a bitch in L.A.?' Ingrid added again.

'Ingrid!!'

'Sorry. But the car *is* waiting,' Ingrid said with a grin.

Julia and I smiled at each other, and then before I knew it, she'd wrapped me up in a tight hug. I squeezed her back and closed my eyes, surprised that I suddenly felt like crying. But if it hadn't been for Julia, I never would have been able to leave my life behind for a little while. I would never have found out that rock stars can be frogs and regular guys can be princes. Or that just cleaning a toilet could be so empowering. Or that taking a ride from a guy named Crazy Dave is *never* a good idea.

Ingrid sniffled and let out a little whimper. 'I'm just so touched by this moment, I think I'm gonna cry.'

I pulled away from Julia and shot Ingrid a look. 'You know, we do still have stockades on the grounds. I've seen 'em.'

Ingrid raised her hands and rolled her eyes, slumping back into the pillows again.

'So, you ready to go back to being a princess?' Julia asked.

I smiled and shoved my hands into the back pockets of my jeans. 'You know, I think I might be able to handle it,' I said. 'What about you? You ready to go back to being a normal girl?'

'Oh, Carina,' Julia said, shaking her head at me with mock seriousness. 'That's the one thing you just didn't understand about me. I was *never* a normal girl.'

She winked at me once, then turned and fluttered her fingers at Ingrid and glided out of the room, doing an extreme exaggeration of my walk.

'Freak!' I shouted after her.

'Princess!' she shouted back, clearly halfway down the stairs. I laughed and looked at Ingrid.

'She's certifiable,' Ingrid said, toying with the fringe on one of my pillows.

'You totally *are* in love with Markus,' I said.

'Just a little,' Ingrid said with a wince.

'You are so dead!' I shouted. I launched myself onto the bed and whacked her over the head with one of the beaded pillows.

'Ow!' she shouted, smacking me on the back of the head with another.

We battled and shrieked and shouted until my mother came by my room and paused in front of the door. Ingrid and I froze, totally snagged. My hair was all in front of my face and hundreds of feathers were floating around the room from an exploded pillow.

'Girls, this is no way to conduct yourselves,' my mother said sternly. My heart thumped as I waited for an extension of my grounding. Then my mom reached over and grasped the doorknob. 'At least not with the door open,' she said with a wicked smile.

I grinned as the door clicked closed, and then Ingrid attacked me all over again. As we laughed and ran around the room, dodging and weaving and swinging until I was totally out of breath, I didn't feel like a princess at all. I didn't feel like a normal girl.

I just felt like me.

Epilogue

'Julia! You coming to lunch?' my roommate, Anna, asked as she grabbed her jacket and book bag. I flopped down on my bedspread and pulled out the latest *People* magazine from my bag.

'Nah. I have some reading to catch up on,' I said with a grin.

Anna laughed, her huge smile lighting up the tiny, poster-covered room. 'You're such a nerd,' she said jokingly. 'I'll see you at study group tonight.'

As soon as she was gone, I leaned back into the pillow on my narrow twin-size bed and opened the magazine to the four-page spread right near the centre. I smiled when I saw Carina grinning back at me from under a Yankees baseball cap.

PRINCESS ON CAMPUS, the headline read. I flipped the page and rolled my eyes at a picture of Carina looking all studious and New York as she bent over a notebook at a classroom desk. She was wearing black-rimmed glasses that I was sure were fake and had her hair back in a bun. Her wardrobe was all J. Crew –

wool turtleneck and jeans. I could just imagine the truckload of clothes she'd had delivered to her dorm room at Columbia.

I put the magazine aside and rolled over on my bed, picking up the framed picture of Carina and me that we'd taken that summer at Disneyland. We had posed on either side of Cinderella and couldn't stop giggling. We were such dorks.

Sighing, I pulled a couple of notebooks out of my bag and forced myself to move over to the desk. When I'd applied to Cornell last year, everyone had told me the hard part was getting in, but once I was there, it would be a piece of cake. They had definitely lied. But I loved the work. I loved being there. I loved that I hadn't been forced to take out student loans to attend. My mother's hat business was booming, and she had no trouble coming up with the small part of the tuition that my scholarships didn't cover. But I wasn't letting her pay for everything. I had a work-study job at the library to pay for my living expenses.

And I had about an hour to cram before I had to be there.

I settled into my desk and opened up my world civ book, smiling as I flipped past a section on Vineland. I was just about to get into reading up on the Peloponnesian Wars when there was a knock on my door.

'Perfect timing,' I said under my breath.

I got up and yanked open the door, fully expecting to find my RA, Jasper, scowling at me for not having finished the bulletin board I'd promised to decorate. Instead I was staring up at a face I'd thought I would never see again. My heart stopped beating and I clasped the doorknob for support.

'Markus?'

His smile was as amazing as I remembered. Before I could rethink it, I threw my arms around his neck.

'What're you doing here?' I asked, pulling him into my room.

'Well, I'm checking out the school,' he said. He unfolded a sheet of cream-coloured paper from his pocket and handed it to me. 'I got into the architecture programme.'

I didn't know what to say. We'd e-mailed once in a while over the past two years, but he'd never mentioned even applying for the programme. I sat down on the edge of my bed and almost fell off.

'You're . . . you're going here?' I said.

'In the spring,' Markus told me, sitting down across from me on Anna's bed. He rubbed his hands together and smiled. 'Surprised?'

'Oh, I'm surprised, all right,' I said, my heart pounding out of control. 'Am I ever.'

'Now, I don't want you to get all freaked out. I'm not stalking you or something. This is one of the best architecture schools in the world.'

'Yeah, I know,' I said with a grin. I folded up the letter and handed it back to him. 'Congratulations. How did you . . . I mean . . . I thought your father . . . '

The butterflies in my stomach were going crazy and I actually felt light-headed. Markus was sitting in my room!

His hair was shorter and he was wearing a pair of jeans and a dark sweater and he looked even more incredible than I had remembered.

'You know how I interned at the ministry for a few months and I was so bored and miserable? Well, apparently I wasn't very good at hiding it – even my father noticed,' Markus explained. 'He finally told me that he didn't want to be responsible for my imminent suicide, so he let me send out applications. I didn't tell you before because I didn't want to jinx it.' Markus laughed and shook his head. 'I got into a bunch of places, but—'

'You decided to come here,' I said, blushing.

'Yeah,' he said, looking me in the eye.

'And . . . why was that again?' I teased.

'Well . . . like I said . . . it had nothing to do with you . . .' Markus said, still grinning. He got up and sat down next to me, reaching over and taking my hand. 'Unless, of course, you want it to . . .'

A tingle of warmth shot up my arm as I laced my fingers through his. 'Now, Markus, you should never run your life around love,' I said sternly, trying not to smile. 'If there's one thing I've always believed, it's that you can't let a relationship get in the way of your dreams.'

Markus reached up with his free hand and touched my cheek, turning me to face him. 'But what if you have two dreams, and they both happen to be right in the same place at the same time?'

My heart pounded in my chest as I looked into those hopeful blue eyes. 'Well, then I'd say you are a seriously lucky guy,' I told him.

'No arguments there.'

Markus leaned in to kiss me, his fingertips never leaving my face, and just before our lips touched, we both smiled. I knew that Markus and I were the luckiest people in the world. All of our dreams had already come true, and this was only the beginning.

Look out for:

The Virginity Club

Coming Soon!

Eva, Debbie, Kai and Mandy are best friends. They're also all looking for an escape route from high school – an escape none of them can manage on their own. Which is where Mrs Treemont's scholarship fund comes in . . . but the girls soon discover that being awarded it depends on more than high grades – they've also got to prove they're still virgins. And, in the competition to win the scholarship, the girls are soon playing dirty . . . Is the award worth more than their friendship?

Simon & Schuster
ISBN 068986065X